CW00521099

A MOMENT OF PERFECTION

Emily B. Scialom

A Moment Of Perfection

AUTHOR BIOGRAPHY

Emily Bollington Scialom was born in Hackney, London on July 27th 1984. She spent her childhood years in Glastonbury and then relocated with her family to Cambridge in 1996.

She was a nationally published poet aged 8, an internationally published poet aged 17 and began writing her first novel in 2008.

'The Religion Of Self-Enlightenment' was published by Olympia in 2016 and was declared 'a cult sensation' (Cambridge News) in 2018. This acclaimed work was soon followed by 'The Rivers' (Austin Macauley, 2019), which featured in The London Book Fair and The Los Angeles Times Festival Of Books 2022.

'Eternal Artist' (2020), 'My Searches For Meaning' (2021) and 'Viajes Internos' (2022) were all self-published poetic works which occupied her time during the Covid-19 pandemic.

'A Moment Of Perfection' is, therefore, her third novel and sixth available work.

A Moment Of Perfection

ACKNOWLEDGMENTS

Thank you to my dear friend, William Hartston, for his ongoing editorial efforts. His influence is an undeniably positive one and I have tremendous respect for his invaluable advice.

A Moment Of Perfection

PART ONE:
The Birth Of A Dream

A Moment Of Perfection

Chapter One

The backstreets of London jangled with emotion as word spread of a new arrival for the Keith family. "It's a boy!" came the cries from relatives, friends and locals, who jostled for space around the small dwelling to pay their respects and watch the day's events unfold. It was quite a commotion for the young household, but the crowd were mostly glad to hear that new life had arrived safely and no pre-existing life had been taken.

"Congratulations all round," rang the unanimous praise from all quarters. It was the morning of February the 3rd in the year 1703 and England's capital city was awash with blessings and troubles. Elijah Francis Keith was born in a ramshackle part of the city, in a dilapidated house to a family already distorted by grief.

His mother, Jane Sarah Keith (nee Smith), had been a seamstress all her life, repairing diligently whatever torn garment was set before her. But at that very moment, she held a brand new bundle of flesh and bones, knowing not what to do with it; however, she still wanted to leap for joy.

9

Jane was a small woman, slight of frame and diligent of mind. With her almond hair and infectious smile, her charm was in the subtlety of her beauty. Her surface fragility belied an inner strength which few could claim to match. She had lost two children already: Elizabeth, in childbirth, and a boy, Francis, during a particularly bleak winter in a city regularly afflicted by fire and disease. She fretted at every gust of wind during the first year of Elijah's life, but he could not have been more protected.

Elijah's father, James Edward Keith, made his money through less than desirable means, often at cards or other such endeavours of the night. Matching the height and build of almost every other man they came across, James became unremarkable in the company of more than a handful of macho types. Robust and sturdy, he knew his way around in a fight, prowling and jerking with all the tension of an animal uncaged.

Indeed, James felt a kinship with fighters, aggressive and hungry as he was for confrontation. His temper was a thing to be feared by even the roughest of men and trouble was his loyal companion.

James became tired of his familial duties since marrying and experiencing the heartbreak of losing two children; he was absent from Elijah's birth. No one knew where the winds of desire and confusion had taken James, but when he was found and brought home he had given his son's name with difficulty in writing to distant relatives such was his inebriated state. Wobbly of hand and clumsy of mind his words came fragmented, as though written by a bad author.

"Where's James?" Jane had asked with trembling lips during the most intense moments of her pregnancy. This question had been echoed during the birth itself. Very few knew the answer, and those who did were loath to share such sordid gossip. Thus Elijah came into the world as a one-winged plane, devoid of the father figure he would spend most of his life seeking.

Despite the negligence of his father, Elijah's mother filled her position with style and grace, taking on most of the family chores and, eventually, financial burdens. Jane looked upon Elijah in those early days when it was so often just the two of them as Mary must have gazed upon the baby Jesus: Elijah seemed a blessed presence in her life. It would be nice to have a young man about the house eventually, someone to protect and serve her, even to follow her into the great battle of life.

Half of Elijah was, therefore, stubborn and strong-willed while the other half was sensitive and soft as the light of a dying day. Though his eventual disposition remained unclear, Elijah was a cherished child; and his impoverished parents gave him everything they could to ensure his childhood was not filled with the futility of an already-wasted life. At a financial push he was given tuition in languages and practical skills at a young age, and relished the opportunity to learn and develop far beyond the limitations of his peers.

"What is 'how are you?' in Spanish?" the boy enquired to his mother one morning in the summer of 1709.

But Jane had not a clue.

"You're getting too clever for me, Elijah. Too clever by half!" She had first said this to Elijah when he was aged just six and her son would continue from that point to torment her with questions she couldn't answer. Such existential interrogations always summoned the same response.

Elijah's brother, Thomas, had been born two years after him and, though their stars were of different constellations, they immediately formed a close bond even beyond blood and familiarity. As a result they were inseparable for years, learning and growing together in peaceful harmony. The troubles of their lives were always shared, whether it be their father's behavioural issues or their mother's at times unsettled mental wellbeing.

Each child had his own characteristics, yet they seemed somehow to complement one another in the most remarkable way. Where Eli was carefree and thoughtful, Tom was practical and straight-forward.

While the boys grew increasingly close during their formative years, their parents drifted further apart. The couple had differing views on how to raise children, a tragic situation that only became apparent while they were in the midst of the process.

Jane was a sympathetic creature, forgiving and comforting rather than hostile. James interpreted this softness as weakness and claimed that the household suffered from a lack of discipline. The patriarch may have thought of himself as a source of order and structure, but Jane thought him savage.

On several occasions James would raise his hand to the boys with only Jane's form intercepting the blows. This aspect of her husband's character was a source of endless confrontations between the two, disturbances which the children could hear through the paper-thin walls with little space to manoeuvre.

As his parents became more fraught in their relations, the brothers grew inseparable, going through times of joy and sorrow as one vehicle of familial attachment. They shared stories of romance and education as they matured within their humble abode, and never allowed a competitive thought to enter into the union.

The Keiths lived in a simple brick house with two rooms. Though cramped and in a state of disrepair, even this abode was rather a stretch for the family as they would discover in the coming years.

As Elijah grew to be a small but robust young man he was allowed to roam the streets with increasing leniency on the part of his parents. The sights which met him during his strolls around the local area incited much confusion in the adolescent's mind. The population of London soared past 600,000 during Elijah's youth and Stuart Britain had many festering social and economic problems. Orphans and destitute beggars were commonplace on the filthy, crime-infested streets while the early workhouses were a constant threat to the poor and vulnerable.

Elijah began to ask the kinds of questions which had no immediate answers regardless of one's intelligence and worldliness: why were some born to great fortune while others' lives were bare? Why were grace and common decency as qualities so rare, as though they were diamonds hidden amidst the rocks of everyday ignorance and cruelty?

Many of Elijah's acquaintances found themselves swallowed whole by a life of servitude and desperation. Even from a tender age the Keith's elder son became wary of close relationships with his peers, lest he know the heartbreak of separation too often.

15

Queen Anne was on the throne at Elijah's birth, ruling from 1702 to 1714. It was a time of extraordinary cultural change and development; Scotland and England merged during her reign in 1707 as a result of the Acts Of Union and an in some ways superficially united Britain emerged from the political upheaval.

Elijah knew little of such colossal geographic changes, but when George I ascended the throne in 1714 he learnt a little more of his rulers thanks to his father's furious disapproving rants.

"I can't believe we're ruled by such a scoundrel!" James would exclaim at dinner when he was present and sober for long enough to comment on such affairs.
A disreputable and wildly unpopular monarch, it was said the first native German to rule England could not speak English and mistreated the women with whom he formed close connections.

His father's complaints were ironic to little Elijah, who had begun to notice the shortcomings in his own familial unit: James seemed quick to judge others and slow to criticise himself, but such is the way in life as Elijah would grow up to find.

The Keiths were no royalists: the transitions of such powerful figures were celebrated with all the flair and devotion of strangers' birthdays. Indeed the combination of an excuse to get drunk and the ascension of a succession of loathed figures proved to be overwhelming to the young man Elijah now found himself to be: scenes of debauchery and confrontation between his parents often marred the occasions of mass celebration.

His mother began to dread such conflicts and would mostly keep her opinions to herself lest one of them offer further cause for refutation. The constant hum of revolution and civil unrest was at times deafening; a tidal wave of ill will and conflict was seemingly forever threatening to crash upon the shores of their lives.

The external commotion was mirrored internally by the strained relationships within the family. However, Elijah had one irreplaceable memory of Thomas from his early years; a memory which delighted him no matter what stage of life he had got to or into what scenario he had been conjured; you can haunt without having died.

17

It was the summer of 1711 and Thomas had awoken with a start. He had a dream about drowning, gurgling and speechless, he floundered for life. At the moment he died he awoke to find himself in a pool of his own urine. Embarrassed, ashamed and powerless against the judgements of those who would condemn him, Tom collapsed in floods of youthful tears.

Rolling and thrashing around on his bed, the limits of the younger brother's emotional world had been reached. Flowing and streaming down his face came the tears of deep shame for what he had done unconsciously, without autonomy.

Though their parents slept soundly, upon hearing his brother's sobbing Elijah came to. Sleepy and confused, he tried to focus his bleary eyes. Elijah looked from Tom's simple bed to his remorseful, tear-soaked face and instantly recognised his own course of action. Eli began to pull his underwear down and then urinated all over his own bed. "See, now we're both in trouble!" he remarked with sympathetic glee.

Tom had stopped whimpering and lifted his head. Upon seeing his brother's urine-soaked

18

bedding he immediately felt better and, although it was a pain for their parents to clean up once they awoke, it eventually brought them closer still: embarrassments and triumphs were always to be shared from that point onwards in equal measure.

Chapter Two

Despite Elijah's fondest recollections, his childhood was marred by frequent unsavoury incidents. Many nights he and Thomas would find their mother crying, weeping uncontrollably at some secret misdemeanour of their father, who was absent from the scene in order to avoid blame and reprimand.

As the boys grew older they began to understand more, and their view of their father became distorted with the aching and yearning of their mother for a better man in her life. Each time James would disappear a fresh wound would open up in the family, a new set of circumstances to mull over or avoid thinking about entirely.

Was he with another woman? Was he drunk in an alehouse or visiting creatures of the night? In truth, no one really knew. All the children comprehended was that their father wasn't there to provide shelter, comfort and a guiding hand to the burgeoning family.

It took Thomas only a few years of childhood to begin his own forays into rebellion. Soon he, too, was found in alehouses and dragged home.

Soon, he too was taken to prisons and not released without beatings.

Elijah found himself increasingly alone in the world, and began throwing himself into studies and imaginary adventures within his mind. He also began keeping diaries at a young age, making notes of the lessons he learnt and the changes he went through with a passion which belied his inexperience.

Sometimes, in isolation with his thoughts, he would create characters who sailed the open seas and never came back, an eerie feeling seeping through his being, a prescient awareness of the grand possibilities life presents to adolescents. He never got in trouble with the law – or anyone for that matter. He would rather keep himself to himself and drift off into imaginary worlds filled with mystery and the great unknown; in short, he had become a true dreamer.

Many times he would draw in notebooks or sit staring into space, wondering how to escape the asylum he called home. His one true source of reassurance and grace was his dear friend William, with whom he had grown up, shared streets and, later, confided his stories to.

William was an avid listener; he listened to the birds, the stories of his friends and the rumours on the streets.

He was a special boy, sensitive and emotional as childhood days were long. Unremarkable to look at with his mousey brown hair, hazel eyes, average height and build, his real calibre shone in knowing him. He yearned to please those around him, to keep logic and order even when there was evidently none to be found externally. Furthermore, William sought to find the truth of every broken heart he came across for, seeing so much sadness in the world, he was determined not to contribute to the emotional distress he was exposed to. He sought only reason and right, and in Elijah at that point in time he saw both.

Elijah and William grew together: they lived in the same street, went to the same school and were basically the same age. Although William saw trouble brewing in Thomas' ways, Elijah had become a strong connection to truly treasure.

William's father. Paul, had died in an alehouse brawl when William was just a boy. He missed having a masculine presence in his life every

22

day, sharing a dwelling as he did with his mother, Jill, and two sisters, Mary and Catherine, but he felt sorry for those around him whose fathers were worse than none. Jill, meanwhile, worked hard as a maid in wealthy households for her family. Without a man beside her it was difficult to survive, and poverty was always reminding her of its presence.

Still, William's home life was a stable tragedy compared to the tumultuous experiences of others. There would be terrible rumours about some of his friend's parents on the streets, which William couldn't help but hear. Temptation accompanied every step for some people, their weaknesses for liquor and sex crippling their ability to walk straight and true.

One day William told Elijah the gossip that his father had a mistress and frequented the whorehouses in the centre of the town. When her husband was found, drunk and stinking of deceit, Elijah's mother would drag him back to the family home amidst huge scenes and the discomfort of all witnessing the events. There was an unleashed beast parading itself in Elijah's life, a snarling vicious monster: it was The Truth.

Whenever this monster showed itself there was trouble at hand, and Elijah spent many a sore evening placating his tormented mother after a commotion. Sometimes she would have bruises in hidden places Elijah found only when she fell to the floor and her dress flew up to expose them. It shocked Elijah to see the cruelty of this world, the naked reality of life for a long-suffering woman.

Thomas mostly hid from the troubles, preferring to hibernate in the face of family strife. Jane had no problem with his absences, but Elijah's impositions into her personal life brought retributions.

"Elijah, it's not your business. You keep your head down and focus on your own life. How are your studies going? Tell me what you've learnt recently? I never had an education like yours; I always had to work hard for everything I could call my own. You should be thankful that your father and I have been able to provide for you, and not berate me so for choices which are not your own."

"But mother, father beats you! He cheats! He drinks all day! He makes and spends all of his money on gambling! What are we going to do?"

"None of this 'we' business, my son. It is my business alone. I love your father. We'll make things work for the sake of you and your brother!"

"So I'm to keep my nose out and be on my merry way, yet all you do is for me and Thomas? It doesn't make sense, mother, think of what you're saying. You're allowing him to treat you in such ways and expecting life to just go on without comment. I have learnt a great deal, thanks to you, but this I cannot understand."

Despite his objections, the young Elijah did what he could to help: cooking, cleaning and fetching supplies were regular parts of his upbringing, particularly when Thomas fell in love at a young age and started to vacate the family home.

Lucy, his first taste of young love, was an obnoxious creature to all except Thomas, it seemed: she paid no heed to the family and they, in return, showed her little regard. Thus Thomas was, in his eyes, forced into a life of sneaking and stealing moments and sometimes days with his sweetheart, exploring the wild and untamed outer limits of romantic relations at an age when he should have been merely learning about them from books.

Yet he despised books. It was life itself where real wisdom lay, he intuitively felt for better or worse.

Despite his father's disapproval, James was in no position to raise his voice with reprimands. Jane, in her confusion and gentility, decided to turn a blind eye to proceedings. Thus, the foundations of a future deviant were laid.

Chapter Three

It was a rare event when James' winnings could feed his family, but it did happen on occasion. These times were marked by celebrations marred by trauma. The four of them would sit around a table of fine foods, clandestine tensions bubbling over here and there, trying and failing to have some fun.

"Could you pass the potatoes, dear?" James would ask.

"Yes, darling," Jane replied, obediently serving the head of the household.

"Let's say a prayer before we proceed," James instructed, peacefully.

There was a hushed calm as the young family huddled over their plates and brought their hands together. Elijah could feel the awkwardness brewing within him, though he did nothing to interrupt the pious procession.

"Dear Heavenly Father,

Thank you for the meal we are about to enjoy.

Thank you for providing for your devoted servants.

We ask that you watch over us today and every day.

Keep us safe from harm and protect our every step.

In Jesus' name,

Amen."

At the conclusion of his father's prayer Elijah became tangibly disorientated and confused about life once again. How could his family all be devoted servants to the Lord when they were enjoying the winnings of a gambler? He decided his concerns would be better off expressed.

"Why are we celebrating, father?" came the innocent question.

"Never you worry, son. Just enjoy the food while it's here. God has provided richly for us tonight," James replied, portions of food tumbling onto his napkin with increasing frequency.

"But I want to know where it's come from…"

Elijah forced the point, and an eerie silence gripped the table.

Never one to fuel a confrontation with her beloved children, Jane stepped in to calm proceedings. "Your father has come into some money. He wants to celebrate with us, his loving family. Don't you worry yourself with the details. All that's here is for you to enjoy without further concern, Elijah."

With that comment Elijah's querying came to an end, yet he remained concerned by the friction he observed. Later in the evening Elijah, clearly bothered by the events of the day, asked William what he thought.

Bound by an inner obligation to honesty, William did not hold back. "Your father's a cheat, Eli, in all the ways it's possible to be such a thing."

"I know that, but why does God provide for cheats? It seems somehow wrong, that's all."

"Religion's mad, Elijah. Nothing but hypocrisy and lies. I don't know, eh? Your family and their funny ways. I can't understand why you pay God any mind. Can He see you now? Can you see Him? Do you believe His son, who is Him

29

as well, died for the sins you have yet to commit? No, forget it. Not for me. I will never understand it."

Elijah replied: "You'd better watch your tongue, William. Thoughts such as those will get you into trouble one day, if you're not careful. Besides, don't you think it's funny that in every culture the world has ever known there are new beliefs in the afterlife, though? I've read about the Gods that people used to pray for. Everyone believes in something."

William was incensed. "Not I! I believe in treating others how you wish to be treated, which is wise and logical, but nothing more. It's all about survival. We've got to live good lives, try to improve the world we find ourselves a part of and use the opportunities we have to better ourselves and make a family," he paused. "Your God willing," he added, with a wicked smile.

Elijah disagreed. He said, "I believe in the God that watches over me and my mother, but I can't see God's work in the ways of my father. He does nothing except complain all day, which for a saved man is unbecoming."

"Haha!" William roared. "You think your father's

saved!" He doubled over in waves of giggles. "That's the funniest thing I've ever heard!"

At this Elijah left the room in his best friend's home and was chased down the street by the mockery of his supposed ally. Eventually Elijah turned round and attacked his friend, laying him low on the floor and wrestling with William until his laughter had calmed.

"SHUT UP! SHUT UP!" Elijah repeated as he bent and bowed William into submission. "Don't ever say my father's not saved again!"

"You're mad, Elijah! Religion has made you mad! Your father's not saved any more than the whores at the docks! I'm not saying he's going to Hell. I just think he should treat your mother better!"

"Well, that's the sanest thing I've heard in a long time. Try telling her that – she's blind with love!"

They made their peace and continued on their journey through the streets of London together, never leaving one another's side despite their growing differences as people. It was a hard life together, let alone apart, and neither of them wanted God, of all things, to come between them.

Elijah wondered if their friendship could withstand such violent storms, yet in resigning some thoughts to inexpression they managed to build a strong foundation against whatever life might throw at them.

Chapter Four

Elijah, surrounded by the multi-cultural tornado of London and in the prime of his early youth, mixed with people of all creeds and tribes. He developed a taste for adventure in the presence of the exotic. The centre of the city smelt like danger, and he was often privy to horrific scenes of violence, prostitution and other unsavoury aspects of life in one of the big trading capitals of the world.

Down by the docks was where trouble resided; if it wasn't in the drinking dens, it would be found down the back alleys which wove themselves through the city with all the intricacy and menace of a dangerous spider's web. The boys often sensed themselves to be innocent prey for the more adult forces of existence which surrounded them. Many didn't make it out of childhood, consumed as they were by work or disease. Elijah learnt to say goodbye to those he had cared for from a young age, a skill he would be forced to hone in later life.

Elijah's beloved mother, Jane, had gained a reputation in her profession as a seamstress by the time Elijah was seven years old, and was finally able to provide them with the gifts they had yearned for so long. Thanks to her diligence, Elijah was educated enough to know a little of the outer realms, and in his youth and adolescence spent many evenings poring over whatever information he could find about the wider puzzle he was a part of.

Elijah's appetite for experiences outside of the norm came early. He would often interrogate the passengers of ships as they arrived, asking where they had come from or where they were going to. Some had come from the unknown world, and this excited Elijah immensely. He began to desperately want to know what it felt like at the edge of the known world, and would speak with William about what he had found.

"Some had come from the New World, William! Do you know where that is?" Elijah exclaimed to his childhood friend while conjuring a map he had stolen from drunk sailors at the dock one evening. He felt bad about stealing, as The Bible told people not to take from unwitting people; his thirst for knowledge overwhelmed his morality at times, just like the first man, Adam.

Laying the map out on the table, he established the existence of many places he was now familiar with:

"Here's The Kingdom of France, Spain, Italia…"

William interrupted. "Where did you find this?"

Elijah continued. "Germania, Portugal…."

William continued his train of thought. "It looks very expensive."

Elijah was in a fit of excitement. "The Netherlands, Bulgaria…"

William finished his trail of thought. "Maybe we could sell it?"

At this Elijah looked at him in disgust.

"This is worth more than a few coins, William. It holds the secrets of the known world! Do you know what comes after this?"

Elijah howled at him, pointing furiously to the edge of the world map. William looked at his feverish friend blankly.

"No, neither do I! And I need to! William, I need to!"

35

Elijah collapsed in a heap in the nearest chair, the weariest teenager the world ever knew. Burdened by expectations of things to come, he felt overwhelmed with emotions before his life had even really begun.

"Maybe we can go there one day?" William said after a long pause; an almighty chasm, it seemed as though the entire universe was sighing.

Chapter Five

It was deep in the night in the Keith household on Hope Street and even the animals that roamed the city by day had found a place to reside. There was a knock at the door of the family home. It was in the midst of winter in 1718 and London was eerie in the blackness. Jane knew it was not a friend for it was too late – only the ghosts were out, haunting the passageways of the ancient city and frightening the perceptive. She lit a candle and cautiously ventured outside.

After opening the door Jane immediately saw a stooped figure rustling some papers. It was only later that she noticed others lurking in the shadows.

"Is this Jim's place?"

"No," she lied.

The man fidgeted and looked at his piece of paper. "Says here 14 Hope Street, a residence of James Keith. Perhaps you know him by his formal name?"

"No, there's no one of that name here." Jane

37

immediately sensed trouble.

The visitor, making a poor impression of a gentleman, would not be dissuaded, but was distracted by the bruise on the woman's cheek. He had a sudden bout of sympathy for her, though as he had approached the door he had felt nothing but rage. Yet apathy remained in this new landscape of emotions – even with a bruise covering her head to toe he still had a job to do, and he would complete the task no matter what.

"I'm sorry to tell you this, but you owe us some money. If you can't pay now we will be taking the amount in possessions..." the man trailed off. "Or..." a pause erupted which neither of them could seemingly control "...what we can find...." The gentleman said, gesturing with his arms around his person, towards the house.

"NO!" Jane cried, and decided to change tactics and try honesty. "Look, he lives here," she rustled her night dress nervously as she spoke. "He's just not in. I will tell him you called. He will pay you what he owes, I promise!"

Her speech came out nervously, stuttering and stalling as chicks leaving their nests in the cold of winter. As she was saying the last words of her sentence the man of the night decided he had had enough. Between his initial ill-defined rage and the woman's lying tongue he had reached his conclusions about what must be done.

He shouted loudly at his colleagues, who gathered hastily in the dark, thus waking the whole street - or so it seemed to Jane. She was humiliated and helpless against these rough masculine figures who now barged into her home. Upon the commotion her children began to squeal.

Large pieces of furniture were soon battling among themselves for space down the stairs and inside the cart which would carry the family's previous belongings into the great unknown, marred by stains and affectionate markings left on them as indicators of a former life.

When the debt collectors had finished there was nothing left. Even the mattresses the children slept on had been taken. For weeks they slept on the floor as Jane took on extra work to pay for replacements. All superfluous classes and outgoings ceased in the face of such painful financial uncertainty.

It was a humiliating experience and Jane promised the children it would never happen again. Her seemingly thankless role as protector and provider was beginning to unravel and she knew that she must act in order to stop the rot.

Chapter Six

It was this incident with the bailiffs which finally convinced the seamstress that she needed to make a change. In early 1719, just as Elijah turned 16, the family moved to Essex without James, who stayed in family homes or mistresses' houses when he wasn't locked up for some misdemeanour or other.

Thomas reluctantly came with his mother and brother, but was never the same again. Lucy, the love of his short life, had become an integral part of all his days. He cried and screamed at the thought of leaving his romance behind, but - like his father - soon found comfort in the arms of another young girl, Emma.

Elijah couldn't understand the charm of his brother, being always the rogue younger sibling to him. The older brother had been much more cautious in his relations with the opposite sex, only moving forward when the circumstances seemed right and entirely favourable.

To her credit, Emma was a sweet and gentle creature, yet she came across as emotional and easily manipulated. Her meeting with Thomas had been akin to a bird with a broken wing encountering a hungry fox: he needed her, but she really didn't need him. Still, in the early days neither was aware of this: the dynamics of their long-term relationship were a mystery they were both in the midst of discovering.

At the wildly tender age of fourteen Thomas moved out of the family home, beginning a new life for himself after he got Emma pregnant and refused to leave her. In some ways Elijah was proud of his brother for finding the courage within himself to meet his fate directly, and not shying away from the responsibilities which would obviously accompany his latest role in life.

The younger sibling soon moved back to London, Emma having come from a wealthy family who had dwellings in the city. However, he then confided in Elijah that his first love, Lucy, was still in his life. At this, Elijah had distanced himself from the inevitable chaos that was to follow, and left his brother to fend for himself in the wild environment of his bad decisions.

Like his father before him, Thomas began to get in trouble with the law, and when James heard about this he threatened to beat the boy to within an inch of his life. Elijah realised his father was disappointed that his youngest son had followed in his footsteps, but Thomas was never present or accountable enough to receive his punishment, instead preferring to re-enact the themes of betrayal and instability that featured so prominently in his upbringing with a dreadful sense of inevitability.

Chapter Seven

The warmth felt soothing on Elijah's back as he lay sunbathing in the garden of his new family home. He was surrounded by drinks and other comforting paraphernalia, occasionally reaching for things to ease his growing agitation.

He was sixteen years old and his mother had just moved him away from London to the leafy suburbs of Essex, though deep down he still felt himself a Londoner. The breakdown of his parents' relationship had signalled an identity crisis in the adolescent boy's mind and he found himself in lonely hours re-shaping and re-moulding the foundations of his broken heart.

His diaries were by then a source of solace and inspiration. He wrote regularly, weaving his stories of fiction and fact until both seemed interchangeable. He considered his family life regularly, his comprehension of pleasure and pain evolving with each passing year. A sense of anger and frustration became familiar in his palette of emotions as he yearned for a better world to emerge.

James was by then a chronic alcoholic, desperate and searching, using drink as a crutch on which to lean his ineffable pain. Theories abounded as to what had caused his deep-seated problems, but it seemed obvious to Elijah that his father struggled most with the business of being alive. It was the drudgery, the day to day battles, which scarred and brought him low. He reached for bottles as a nurse reaches for medicines; the slow, stammering decline of the disenchanted.

His parents before him had provided a seemingly stable environment for James to develop; no one could understand where his obvious suffering stemmed from. He grew up an only child. Carol and David Keith worked hard all their lives, sewing the tapestry of their colourful days as best they could for themselves and their offspring.

Carol worked as a chambermaid and David bought and sold horses used mostly for transport. This work sometimes took David further afield than was comfortable, and perhaps his parents' frequent absences owing to work and leisure had fuelled James' wayward behaviour. However, they had merely desired to put food on the table and keep a roof over their young family's head. No one could see at the time how the future would turn out.

45

In enjoying their lives, it was possible that the Keiths had missed the warning signs of their child's struggles. It took only a little time for James' aggressive character to show itself and, despite having the best intentions, things often fell apart: James would get into trouble at school even before the gang violence started. Meeting Jane had temporarily put an end to that, yet as an animal caught in a trap James found it difficult to free himself from previous habits.

In later life James never spoke of his youth or family much, preferring to concentrate on the immediate. He became estranged from his parents, who regularly wondered what they had done to deserve such excommunication. They even turned up at the door of the Hope Street residence once, but despite the obligatory pleasantries exchanged at the home's entrance there was no way James would permit them to stay for more than a few fleeting minutes.

Jane didn't want to pry, but thought it strange for a man to cut off his loved ones so brutally. Did James not have a heart? She worried that he would end up a lonely old man; she had tried her best to hold on to him, at least.

As Elijah now watched the rich emerald green
of the grass in a sun-drenched haze he noticed
an ant coming across his eyeline. As it wasn't
bothering him there was no debate about
whether or not to kill it, but the scenario
unfolding before him suddenly began to move
him.

The ant, a tiny and seemingly insignificant
creature, was carrying the body of another ant.
Every few paces the mobile animal would drop
the body, search around and return to the
twisted, still carcass.

It occurred to Elijah as he watched the scene
that the creatures were performing a funeral.
Again he watched as the living ant picked up
the body, carried it a few paces and then
dropped it to investigate the surrounding area.
Watching this sorrowful procession a well of
feeling was suddenly sourced within Elijah, a
premonition perhaps of his own traumas, and
he began to cry.

Elijah realised that there was a whole other
world beneath his feet – he may even have
been responsible for the deceased ant's
demise. Who knows how many of these

mournful ceremonies had been performed as a result of his ignorant footsteps and actions? He contemplated the scene and expanded his young consciousness to the point where he could see the interconnectedness of all beings, the suffering that all living things must universally endure.

Chapter Eight

At this point in his young life Elijah was like the salt of the Earth, except in some ways more like a diamond. He shone to all who knew him. As he grew into the man he would eventually become, his knowledge of good and evil seemingly stemmed from many lifetimes. Incarnated in this world of pain and grief, he fought hard to see the flowers and not the metaphorical and literal bodies in the mud. It was so easy: love and allow yourself to be loved. All too often people fell into traps of viewing the world as overly brutal, but even in his very lowest moments Elijah felt there was beauty to be found.

For some the trials and tournaments of life left them dizzy; Elijah saw straight, clearly and truly. His was a mind used to navigating rough seas and, though his experiences didn't break him, they had indeed brought him to his knees. The mind was a riddle he solved with some effort, as others resigned, forfeited or guessed their way into trouble.

Elijah approached life as The Bible says to: with all the innocence and curiosity of a child. He was fascinated by the stories of Job, Moses and

Abraham, the historical tales of intense perseverance and the overcoming of mortal limitations. In a simpler sense, he was forever picking up stones and investigating the shadows, asking "Why?" when others hadn't thought to. To him the world was enough to justify belief in an afterlife: all these miracles falling like dominos to the present moment! How could it be, if not by God?

Of course he had his crises of faith, his tears in the night, his falls from Grace. But he never let them beat him into submission. He saw his faith as his greatest quality, although like minds were sometimes hard to find.

Elijah was focused and decisive: his hands were to be God's hands, only touching what was pure and true, though it was rare to find. Naturally he made mistakes and fell short of the mark, sinning perhaps in his blood. But his intention? Elijah's intention was a clear night's sky and a blanket of stars: he wanted to know The Truth.

Chapter Nine

It was during his formative years in Essex that Elijah really mastered many of the arts of survival. He lived in a small village not far from the crowded streets of Colchester and would often venture far afield on fishing trips, camping expeditions and walks. The river Colne provided the perfect refuge when he was feeling lost and confused; it reminded him of the Thames, which it was connected to, though his past now seemed a distant dream.

He found new friends to keep him company. Tony and Michael were the most loyal to him, although they shied away from matters of the heart, rarely talking of anything but their immediate present. Together they would fish and climb, sourcing beauty where others saw bleak wilderness.

In Colchester he saw the spoils of great trades, the history that pervaded the very walls of the city requesting him to study it. A pupil of the past he found himself, devouring books on the Romans, Celts and the struggles between them.

Boudicca became a prominent figure in his journey through the past as he admired the tenacity and feral ambition of this great woman. Commanders of sea and land also took his fancy, survivors of great battles and the scattered visionaries who led life forever forward.

He didn't dwell on why these stories appealed to him, preferring to drink in the world in a clumsy yet passionate manner. He was a precocious student of life, knowing from a young age how close death would always be to the living and determined to beat the odds.

He thought often of his two siblings who had passed away and wondered who would be next to feed the great beast of disease and strife. It was a wonder he was here at all, he pondered, as he soaked up every minute of his presence in the world.

Chapter Ten

After Elijah moved to Essex, he and William grew from boys into young men, yet still kept in touch. Jane was eventually even making enough financially to send Elijah to London to reconvene with his old friend, so long as he stayed with his Aunt Mary, who remained in the city. Little did Jane know she was sowing the seeds for his departure from her world.

Jane fretted and toiled at all hours of the day and night to make ends meet. It was even the case that in working so devotedly she left herself no time to enjoy the spoils. It was always the case that there was one more garment to be repaired, one new dress to create. She threw herself into her work until her demons had no time to play.

Pleased that Elijah, at least, had time to enjoy his life, she was more than happy to support him with his trips to the capital and quest for camaraderie. William was a lovely boy, and Jane was proud of her son for forming a close connection which rarely showed any signs of frailty.

On occasion Jane would think of the past, a vague sense of cloud approaching as she did so. As a result, she would run from her own thoughts at every opportunity, though they chased her down the back streets of her mind.

Jane hadn't anticipated an adult life mostly spent enquiring about her husband's whereabouts, but here she found herself, still wondering. She felt the absence of James keenly and still strangely held a place in her heart for the man who had broken it. Sill, life was better now, she told herself, proud of her humble accomplishments.

Elijah grew straight as an arrow. He saw the distortions and trials of his youth and he raised the stakes still further. He was determined to contribute something to the society around him, not to just be a taker in a world of insatiable greed. However, his vision remained blurry and the specifics of his plans were hard to identify.

Years passed without dramatic incident. Then one day in 1722 Elijah found his mother crying once again. Jane had received word from her sister, Mary, that his father had been sent to prison for five years for theft and other repeated offences. As James was a known criminal to those who enforced the law the verdict, though brutal, came as little surprise to Elijah. However, he ultimately felt adrift from his familial support network and life changed dramatically.

Jane, now the sole breadwinner and source of emotional support for the troubled young family, often sent Elijah to stay with his grandmother who also lived in the recesses of Essex. Having been part of the justification for moving, Anne Smith became a key part of Elijah's upbringing from this point on along with his Aunt Mary in London.

He would remember the long summer days spent gardening at his grandmother's house for the rest of his life, the kindness that was shown to him echoing through the years. Anne had an endearing sense of humour which Elijah appreciated and fell back on in life's more serious moments.

"Don't let your dreams drown you, Elijah. Keep your feet on the ground even though you seem to have been born with your head in the clouds," Anne would say to her grandson on many occasions. The young man felt seen through by his elder, but mostly ignored her advice as young people are prone to do.

The stresses and strains of trying to raise two children alone were taking their toll on Jane, who spent many a restless night wondering how things could go on. When she finally laid her head down at the end of a long day she felt ambivalent about the prospect of another one. Danger seemed all around and, though it no longer resided in her bed, she became acutely aware of the risks involved in relating to anyone. People seemed somehow too cruel for her, too selfish and unreliable. She had started to lose faith in the human species.

Despite it all things ticked on and Elijah got his first job mucking out stables. He enjoyed the work, the independence and sense of community. For a time peace of mind was a currency he was rich in, but every now and again he had an ominous feeling that things would somehow go wrong. He didn't know where it came from, he just never felt complacent when he found himself in a state of contentment.

Then all at once it happened: Elijah's mother became sick in the winter of 1726. As Jane grew increasingly unwell she tried to maintain her daily routines and provide for her disparate offspring, sending money to Thomas when she could and advising Elijah in the pursuit of his lofty dreams, but it soon became clear that it was an insurmountable task. The doctor was called after her condition worsened and she was diagnosed with smallpox.

The deterioration of his mother's condition had taken Elijah by surprise: at first it was nothing, just a cough and a fever, and then suddenly she was bed-ridden, whispering her last words in her eldest son's ear.

"Elijah, live a full life. Never be blinkered in terms of how things should be. Never presume that just because something is so, it is right and just and will ever be so. Life changes us, but I want you to know your dreams and not be tormented by images which will never come to pass."

Elijah felt like his dreamer-self had been seen through once again. Was there nowhere to hide? It seemed true then what he had heard people say: no one knows you as well as your mother.

"Never look down when you feel yourself getting too high, always look up when you feel yourself getting too low. Keep leaning towards the light of love and all will be well. Live your highest version of your highest self, Elijah, and don't live a life of suffering as I have. Learn to live with the pain of loss and move on in your own time, in your own way. I will be forever beside you, my beloved."

And with those words, Jane departed the world, leaving Elijah grief-stricken at her bedside. After a few relatively stable years Elijah's whole world came crashing down. His Aunt Mary had informed him that Thomas was once again in prison, their father had been nowhere to be found for years, and Elijah had been warned to stay away from his mother for fear of infection. However, his last gesture to her was to disobey this order and keep her body company as her soul travelled to the afterlife.

The tears flowed down Elijah's face as his mother was no more for this world. He knew he had lost a part of his life – a part of himself – which would never live again. It was up to him to make a go of his life and heed the sweet woman's final words to her eldest surviving child.

Elijah immediately felt the urge to run, to get as

far away from this scene and these emotions as he possibly could. He sensed a net of sadness would soon slip over him if he stayed, and he knew just who to talk to. He travelled to London on a miserable journey, repressing the urge to cry for most of the winding way.

He saw William amidst the crowd at the coach station and they immediately made their way to a more private setting. William knew there was serious trouble at hand, but during the elucidation of recent events he would be troubled more than he could say. The truth seeped out of Elijah in fits and starts, tears welling in his reddened eyes.

"William, my mother's died."

William was quiet as he sipped his beer in his unease. Now a 23-year-old with a strong sense of empathy, he reached out through his words to comfort his friend. "I'm so sorry, Elijah. Your mother was a wonderful woman. She deserved so much more from this world. Is there anything I can do?"

"You can help me arrange the funeral."

So they did just that. A week later, in the

pouring rain and the freezing wind, Jane was buried in a local Essex cemetery. The tears mingled with the rain as they laid her coffin down, and Elijah felt a pain in his heart unlike any other he had experienced. They dressed in well-meaning uniforms of black and watched as Jane's body was laid to rest in a simple grave which belied her elevated stature in the eyes of many.

William was right by his best friend's side throughout the ceremony, a touch of the arm here or a word or two there let Elijah know he was not completely alone.

That afternoon in the local church William lost sight of Elijah for a minute or two. Searching in a panic, wondering what had occurred, he soon found Elijah praying at the very front of the building. William sat down next to his dear friend in pious silence, hoping not to disturb the intense focus of the bereaved.

"William, I have to go away," Elijah said without looking up, his world falling down around him in slow motion. "There's nothing for me here anymore. I must go as far from this wretched place as I can and never come back!"

"Let me come with you, my friend," came the reply. "You know those dreams you always talked of as a young child? Let's make them happen. There are ships leaving all the time for the New World – the edge of the map you always longed to see. Let us depart on one of them in the New Year."

Thus, they spent a lonely winter in 1726 living together in a small room in London, working when emotions and circumstances allowed. The families they had once been a part of had now fallen away: they were as adrift as human beings could be. But they, at least, had each other.

Chapter Eleven

James, however, had no one. In the dank underground of a squalid London prison - which many felt was his rightful place - the cries of lost souls echoed through the evening air. It was a damp and perilous winter evening, which seemed to want more from him than he could give. He found himself flittering in and out of consciousness like a mosquito connecting painfully with the flame it circled.

The ageing James could feel himself physically disintegrating, wasted muscles buried under slack flesh and bones protruding at peculiar angles. But nonetheless the hopes of the deluded rested in the confines of his blackened heart: he would get out of this cell of regret and retribution one day, he told himself. For now the chains that bound him remained stronger than his grip on life.

Guards came and went, a blur of authoritarian tensions and unwarranted hierarchies. In truth, they were no better than their prisoners, these broken and disturbing men who inflicted violence in excess of the justice they were paid to enforce.

"Get up!" came the merciless cry, hissed with the venom of a vicious reptile or an eagle honing in on its prey. James could do nothing except oblige, though to do so brought pain he had trouble locating - was it his body, mind or soul from which his agony truly sprang?

Raising himself to his feet brought pangs of languishing bruises to the fore; they now mingled with a fresh sense of desperation to be no more. All his life had been a waste. James was the kind of man who had never even attempted to graduate from the fool to the wise man, let alone made the transition. Now justice was being served, yet still James refused the medicine offered through deep reflection and remorse.

He had always done his best - at least that's what he told himself. He was incarcerated as a result of trying to provide for his loved ones, though he knew nothing of their state of being these days: did the world nurture his dear family presently or had it cast them aside as a dog rids itself of lice?

Still he remained, fighting against the tide of self-loathing with his lies and lack of interest in his distorted moral compass. Had he been a good man? Was he now a bad man? The judgement was not his to make, he clumsily concluded.

"What do you want from me?" were the most honest words James had whispered for days; he spoke with all the curiosity of a small child. A blow landed on his cheek in response and any appetite he had for further communication soon dissipated along with the sun's light on this winter night. James had watched it beginning to sink through a small grate in the wall, all but wishing it away.

"Don't speak unless spoken to! I don't know how many times you must be told."

Upon the sight of his prisoner bracing himself for more of the same, the guard's angry tone abruptly changed and became more cheerful. However, the contents of his speech had blackened further and seemed completely disconnected from his fluttering melody.

"You are to go without your meal tonight: your chores were sloppily carried out and in most cases incomplete. Any complaints you can address to your maker," the guard sneered and placed a cup of water on the floor in place of food.

Feeling anger flood his being James could barely bring himself to complain such was his permanent weakness. Another night without food was the least of his worries. He sat back down and counted his woes as the guard left.

Deep in the night as James slept a strange light permeated his vision. Soft, at first, as a far away candle. It crept closer and closer until the light disturbed the sleeping convict, the shameful shell of a once free man. Encaged within these mouldy walls, the darkness was approached by a foreigner and soon James awoke, stirred by the almost luminous commotion.

Blearily conscious, James rubbed his eyes and sanitised his anguish. If this was his death, he surmised, he could at least face it soberly. He rolled as far as his chains would allow to get away from this eerie vision, but as he stared at the light in his cell a strange peace came over his fierce soul. It was a peace he had never before experienced emanating from a light not of this world. Illuminating his starkly empty surroundings, the bars seemed for a moment transcendental and not solid as they were just moments ago.

"What is happening?" James managed to cry, his mask of contentment slipping. The kisses of bliss which arrived on his cheek were enough to make a man into a child.

The speech which soon accompanied such sensations was not so positive, however.

"You must change..." A voice bellowed as a figure stood before him, proud and on the verge of translucent.

James stared, his jaw hanging loose, and wondered. A retrospective glimpse at moments of his past filled his mind, flashes of colour and emotion. He thought he would go mad, but at that moment the light desisted and ceased, it seemed, to be.

He spent all of his allotted proceeding hours dwelling upon the details of the scene. Was he delirious or sick? His pain had seemed to dissipate since the visitation - or was that simply his imagination? His bruises felt somehow lighter and devoid of their previously incessant aching.

In moments such as this you have a choice about how seriously you take things. James decided to tackle with both feet the issues raised.

On what pathway did he find himself? At which point had he taken a wrong turning? One thing was sure: he had become so lost that an angel had been disturbed from his slumber.

A fire stirred in the Englishman's belly, a righteous anger at his own wickedness. If only he could get out of this mental, emotional and spiritual cage he would obey this spirit of the night with all his might!

The very next day another guard came calling, his tone apparently softer than those of his previous colleagues.

"Mister Keith, you are to be freed soon. Eat up, you'll need your strength."

So taken aback was James at his good fortune that he stared at the guard for so long it incited a final beating before he was freed. Whether it be an angel or phantom that had lit up his life,

67

James retained his ability to provoke even the most mild mannered of creatures to violence.

Alone and out in the world once again, he was a driven and hungry man indeed. He had an appetite for goodness only the finest of men could match.

He walked past beggars wishing he had some currency to offer them but kindness. Yet those beggars were now his superiors in the social hierarchy in which he found himself right at the very bottom. No moment of despair overwhelmed him, however. He walked the streets with a spring in his step among strangers who he believed could soon be friends.

There were three incidents in a week which shook James to his very core. The first was an encounter with someone he had wronged in a previous life.

Unbeknownst to James' previous drinking companion this now pious and conscientious man had humbled himself before the altar of love.

"You owe me money, you scoundrel," the bruising Bill intoned.

"I will repay you, I swear it," James returned.

"You'll repay it now, thief!"

A fight ensued which made light of James' treatment in prison.

So James, left once again badly bruised and beaten, was confronted with an ugly past.

The second scene took place when James visited his former sister-in-law, Mary, who never strayed far from her home.

A knock at the door and no one to greet it confused James for a good minute. His wounds were still sore and he groaned at the time spent waiting. Finally Mary answered and felt herself faint, as if visited by a ghost. She swooned slightly before exploding with hatred and accusations.

"I'm so sorry, Mary. I've changed now. I've realised I need to change!" James argued to seemingly precious little effect. These were the magic utterances which meant nothing to Mary

69

at this point, though years ago they would have retained their power: she did not believe him.

Several times she slammed the door only to return with more vitriol. It was during these outbursts that James learnt his wife had died. It was upon receiving scraps of details about his sons' lives that he realised he'd been a bad father.

A passer-by finally intervened and asked Mary what the problem was.

"The problem is that people can beat and abuse all who love them for years and then return many moons later with these pitiful crumbs of remorse expecting to have a civil conversation."

At this James objected, convinced as he was of his newfound innocence.

"The acts of my past are shameful to you and me both - I wish, I only wish, I could erase them. However, change is all I offer with my empty, bloody hands. I know your faith was always stronger than mine, but not anymore, Mary. I pray in Jesus' name you forgive..."

At this Mary's screeching careered out of control and the stranger continued on his way, satisfied that the scene could not be redeemed. "JESUS!? NOW YOU BRING CHRIST INTO IT. HAVE YOU NO SHAME? WHAT DO YOU KNOW OF JEEEESUUS?"

She elongated the syllables of His holy name until they became almost musical and the mockery was not lost on James. He retorted.

"Forgive me or do not forgive me, these changes in me remain. I did not know Jane had passed and it kills me during life to know I will never say sorry to her. But I can say it to you: I was a useless, hopeless, lost fool of a husband, father and man. If anyone deserves a second - a fifteenth - chance that it certainly isn't me. But tell me of my boys, at least! Where may I find them?"

Mary looked him up and down as though disgusted by his maker, distorting her face in an unbefitting sneer. "Elijah is going as far away from you as is humanly possible. Thomas is so much your likeness he could be your shadow. If you know of The Bible you'll know you reap what you sow."

71

"Elijah is leaving? Where does my beloved firstborn intend to go and when? Where can I find dear Thomas and inform him of the error of my ways?"

Mary huffed and puffed, but had no intention of saying much more.

"Good lady, PLEASE!" James was reaching a panicked state, fearing the loss of his whole family in one fell swoop.

"Go and find Thomas and ask him the details. It is not my place to save you or any other haunted soul who knocks on my door. Now away with you and go off into the night from whence you came!"

She would not say more. James left and slept under the nearest tree, a blurry sea of rags and squalor his only company. He awoke the next day pessimistic and full of dread. To change would be his salvation, but any hint of alteration seemed impossible to come by except internally.

He knocked at ex-girlfriends houses and found them gone. He had run ins with officials who recognised him for only who he had been and not who he had become. He wished he had the strength to leave the city and travel to his parents' home, but it was too far out in the country for him to foresee the possibility of completing the journey.

It got to the point where he could barely stumble from step to step, sloping along the streets looking for, beseeching the arrival of, a glimpse of hope. Strangers would take pity on him and throw him some bread or coins if he sat long enough in any given spot. The shame burned along with the gratitude and relief; he knew not whether he wanted to live or die.

Dark nights would surround him and the good days being enjoyed by those who passed him seemed to grind away at his tolerance of a tomorrow. Was life unfair or was this lack of meaning and love exactly what he deserved?

He didn't probe the question for too long, knowing the pressing need for survival lent no moment for indulgence. He wasted days in a drunken stupor, intoxicated by profound grief, confusion and regret.

Some moments pierced his consciousness with all the precision and ill intention of a blade, images seemingly designed to harm him and throw him off course: the first moment he struck his wife, the years of relating to alcohol rather than his own family or self, the foolishness of never finding out how to control his charms. All came back to haunt him in this era of remorse.

Other moments eluded him, a fish in wet hands: where was he when his sons had their 10th birthdays? Where was he when their mother cried? Where were the people he was bound by duty and familiarity to love most now?

The answers had so far escaped him and the road to redemption seemed ever so long. His heart was a broken compass, his tortured soul his only map. He prayed they directed him better than they had before, that he listened intently to any forthcoming spiritual needs with the ears the good Lord gave him.

At last, as though a premonition, James found Thomas in one of the very same brothels he used to frequent. With his emotional vision blurry and his sense of morality skewed, James the family man had often gone looking for trouble in this very establishment - and, mostly, he had found it. Now his son did the same. Thomas was wearing a distinctive beardless look and cheap fancy clothes; his father recognised his youthful good looks on display in his youngest surviving offspring.

Dragging his younger son out almost literally by his ear James found a sense of strength he had not known remained and they fought in the street like cat and dog. Despite his lack of respect for his father, Thomas remained somewhat afraid of him and his volcanic temper, which resembled a force of nature when unleashed as it was now.

The rain came pouring down, the mud in the streets became liquid, the chaos of the natural and the man-made worlds swirled all around them, intermingling though distinct. One had form and balance; the other misery and ruin. Depending on your perspective there was method to the madness, though, and this was the dawn of a society that would one day touch the celestial bodies which orbited the actors as they played their troubled parts.

Lines they had repressed for years tumbled from their mouths, stopping them was a mission neither would accept. It was too late for a sorry and glib explanation: the son was on his way to being as destroyed as his father and only his father himself stood in his way.

"This is no life for you, Thomas. Where is the boy I raised?"

"Can you not see, father? He stands before you exactly as expected. If you wanted a better son perhaps you should have been a better man."

"I am a better man! I don't know what I must do for you or anyone else to see that. Yes, my changes are invisible, mostly involving my character and intentions, but surely these improvements must be of some worth?"

"Improvements? Improvements?! You would need to be an entirely new man for me to ever listen to you!"

At this James grabbed his son firmly and hissed his words with a naked affection for their recipient.

"That I am, boy! I'm more present to your pain and confusion than I have ever been before. I want to talk to you and Elijah in ways I cannot, God rest her soul, talk to your mother any more. Tell me everything, but far away from here."

With this the duo walked as one tortured body, emotions flaring and the constant threat of violence keeping both of them vigilant.

It was during the course of this heartfelt dialogue that Thomas found room to breathe emotionally at last. After confessing all of his pain, he sensed a weight being lifted from his very soul. After all, despite the bravado, he had missed the man responsible for his existence. They talked for hours and came to a harmony between them which had possibly never been reached before. As though a pleasant foreign land, each man navigated this new and seemingly hospitable terrain.

Things changed for James, cogs turned and synapses fired at last in a positive manner. No explosions of guilt and remorse could have been more elegant, but when he asked Thomas about his brother the mood soon shifted.

An icy cold came over the conversation as if confusion now abounded in place of clarity. Thomas agonised internally about how much to say and then finally emitted the truth.

"Elijah is leaving England, father."

"So I've heard," James replied.

"We haven't spoken about why because I have rarely seen him in recent years except by accident, but the truth is he leaves for the New World tomorrow. I realise in sharing this with you that you may try to catch him, but you don't stand a chance even with your strong will and dreams of redemption, so I do not worry too much about telling you."

At this James was startled. In part he was proud of his eldest son for pursuing his grandest dream, but otherwise he was lost in emotions he could not control.

"Why did you not tell me sooner? I must try to tell him my feelings before he leaves these shores forever!"

Recognising the over-reaching of a desperate man Thomas told him the details of his departure and the conversation abruptly ended as James took on his newfound calling.

"I'll be back!" James called over his shoulder as he vacated the scene, though it was unclear whether this was a threat or promise.

Rushing to the edge of England, James persuaded the driver of a horse and cart heading that way to drop him at the seafront using the small amount of coins Thomas had generously given him upon acknowledging the desperation of the man. It was a tangible blessing, despite Thomas' doubts that he would ever make it in time.

Arriving in Southampton James rushed to greet the shore, finding only a bustling crowd preparing to wave off a ship that was soon to depart. He pushed and collided with the often weeping members of the public, and as he got to the front he thought it was too late.

During the journey to Southampton he had spent his time wisely writing a letter he had hoped would be read by Elijah. He managed to confront the very last of the crew who were busily preparing to embark and hurriedly smuggled a letter into one of their hands.

"Is Elijah Keith on this ship?" James directly enquired, desperate for the answer to be affirmative.

"I believe so," replied the sailor, the very same man who had but moments ago read Elijah's name out from the list of departing crew members.

"Please give him this," James replied and handed him the collection of papers which reflected his very soul in their crumpled form.

At the sailor's begrudging agreement James left him to finish his work and stood back to admire the strength and breadth of the vast ship. Elijah's dreaming had led him here, James pondered, and his father gaped in awe at the fulfilment of his son's youthful visions.

Sometimes things get left unfulfilled; a note hung in the air, too lonesome for melody. A moment had passed, but the trail of existential dominoes was now broken and no further movement seemed plausible. James broke down for the first time in his adult life, in front of everybody; he wept bitterly at the sight of his failed quest for complete redemption.

James had indeed changed, but seemingly not quickly enough to save his relationship with Elijah. It pained him to know that his son would remember the person he was without having even an inkling of who he had or would become, and he only hoped his heartfelt words could correct this.

It was true: Elijah had gone to live his dreams while his father was left in many ways in a living nightmare. James had broken somewhere deep inside, but gave his son every blessing for his escape from the sorrow of the known. Whatever happened now James had done his best. Surely that counted for something?

Chapter Twelve

Elijah and William had weeks ago enrolled as crew on the next ship that was going the furthest away from where they were, and the Victoria seemed the most suitable option. Strong and sturdy, she didn't look the sinking type. They concluded that whatever dangers or pleasures lay on the other side, at least they would have a high chance of making the journey.

Largely ignorant of the torment they left behind, the pair and their fellow crewmen departed from Southampton early in the year 1727, verbally stretching and embellishing their dreams of a new horizon each day before their embarkation. No one knew what the future held, but their pasts already seemed foreign to them.

They had run to the docks on the day of departure, physically and emotionally exhausted by the excitement that they pictured before them. Days of sheer adventure, weeks of existential hardship followed by a most rewarding new world to savour at the end of it. That was their dream, anyway.

"Elijah Keith!" came the call, and Elijah had

summoned his paperwork from his pockets.
"William Burns!" soon followed, bellowed from
the ship's side by a slim man with a booming
voice as the crew assembled.

The ship was vast. The huge white sails
billowed from three masts and almost burst in
the wind, yearning as they were for the open
seas to surround them. The men would be
crammed on board in small rooms, with
livestock and supplies separately stored. There
were doctors and medics which the boys prayed
they would not need, as well as true explorers,
ready with their quills and papers to write down
and record anything they saw which might be of
note to those who could not venture beside
them.

As the mist rolled across the English Channel
the boys took their place in the fray with delight.
They climbed stairs, ran hallways and generally
failed to notice the evidence pointing towards a
chain of command they would need to adhere to
in order to avoid trouble. For them it was the
start of their new life and a taste of true freedom
so long denied them by either economics or
geography.

As they stood on board the grand ship, Victoria,

the crew had bid farewell to those watching them from the shore, blowing kisses and whispering well wishes. William had waved to his dear mother who had travelled down to Southampton to see her son depart his motherland and stood nervously on the docks, weeping and trying to hide it simultaneously. Elijah mirrored the motions of the others, yet he knew not who he was waving to.

He had no inkling of his father's aggressive attempts to reach through to him mere yards from where he stood on the ship's stern. Despite their physical proximity the perceived distance between them had, for Elijah at least, never seemed greater.

Chapter Thirteen

The North Atlantic Ocean rolled and swelled beneath the bows of the Victoria. She bent and dragged her way across the sea, encountering waves that were rooted deep in the ocean's currents, a mass of life and death. Tiredness overcame Elijah at times, but when he found a moment he just stared from the deck out into the great unknown and wondered what adventures awaited him on the other side of the world.

It was the beginning of the year 1727 and Elijah Keith was nearing the end of his 23rd year on Earth, just about old enough to have collected enough experiences to stake a claim to adulthood despite the babyface which misled those who looked upon it. His blonde hair danced in the wind and a beard grew unkempt, giving him a weathered look that reflected his inner storm.

Elijah and William had soon been on board for several arduous weeks and the stench of failure was all around them. Failure to clean, failure to cope and, at times and in some cases, failure to survive. The crew had brought some animals with them in order to have a fresh supply of meat, but the creatures had carried their own perils of disease and upkeep.

Travelling with Elijah and William was a crew of no more than fifty men, some of whom they had come to call friends. Jack Drake was the Captain of the vessel, though he remained supercilious in person and strangely out of reach to the mere deck sweepers and chefs. Commands would come down a grapevine and be enacted to the best of the men's abilities, though some would perish in the white heat of authoritarianism and all felt the inconsequential nature of their pulses.

Elijah had simply wanted to get away, though; from the confines of life in middle England to the expectations of his family and friends he felt stifled of the freedom to find and be his true self. On this journey he had promised himself never to return to the doldrums of a life in the mire of others' opinions, and he found himself now breathing in the salty air as though it was his source of all strength and will to live.

His sense of loneliness was sometimes his only company, and as the predatory birds flew high above the whispering sea, it shook him how competent he had been forced to become in order to endure the turbulence of the past few weeks, the depths which he had been able to reach within himself in order to push forwards. Many had not found such resources, and bodies scarred internally and externally had been strewn across the path they had forged between the waves.

He said goodbye to the lost souls in his own way, thinking of all those he had known and loved but were no longer beside him. Death's lingering touch was clearly felt, a firm grasp sensed relentlessly by his mind, body and soul.

His purpose had been to escape the restrictions of his life back home, to find a new land filled with hope and the unknown. However, this aim had been pulled apart and questioned so many times that he now felt himself as adrift as the Victoria in its, at times, seemingly rudderless meanderings through time and ocean.

Often his dreamtime and wonderings were interrupted by shouts from above or below, cries filled with the desperation to stay alive and the nervousness of those on the edge of life and death. No, it was not an easy journey and Captain Drake had outwardly predicted as much many moons ago.

Watching the heavenly bodies circle and change shape and form during their travels had been one of the joys of the experience so far. Yet those same orbiting wonders had borne witness to such suffering and tragedy that Elijah had come to scorn their indifference.

Alone in unforeseen circumstances, like the Victoria, Elijah was doing his utmost to keep afloat in rough seas of inner strife and confusion. He had left all he had known to follow his dreams; he had found nothing so far, except fear and confusion. Yet, without the fulfilment of this yearning in his very soul, Elijah could not turn around. There was only one way to progress and that was to move forward, pushing boundaries wherever he found them and awaiting the arrival of further allies.

He thought often of the afterlife, the wonders of knowing the truth of his soul and the purpose of these struggles. Having grown up a Christian, he soon realised that a creator was most definitely the source of all he touched and saw.

Elijah recalled his early communication with the divine with much joy. There was so much less to worry about as a child; the perils of adulthood had begun to startle and overwhelm him and, increasingly, he leant on his belief in a higher power in order to emotionally sustain himself.

This keen religious fervour, coupled with his extensive youthful Biblical exegesis, had given him the faith to prevail in many a dark moment. He had wondered, sighed and cried aloud into the darkness regarding his deepest fears when alone, and had always felt that his ability to survive suggested he was part of some greater plan for his life. If only he could see it, he would beg in lonely and winding hours beneath deck, struggling and failing to find blessed sleep.

When Elijah did manage to sleep his visions were filled with death and despair. Recurring dreams of his mother haunted him while he lost all appetite for the tasks he was required to complete. There seemed no respite from his anxiety and suffering except through prayer, which was his only passage to contentment.

He would spend as much time as he could find in deep contemplation of life's mysteries; in giving his fears and concerns to the God he so passionately believed in he found he could continue with the brutality of this life on Earth.

Rightly or wrongly, Elijah felt hope for a brighter future and he was determined to survive long enough to see it.

Chapter Fourteen

The wind howled and the rain poured down on the Victoria as the worn vessel made its way uneasily forward.

"William, we have come so far. Will we ever see home again?" Elijah pondered aloud to his beloved friend amidst the storm.

"I doubt it, Elijah. Not much to see there, anyway."

Elijah had a rush of memories flood his mind, images flickering like a dying candle in the wind, thousands of moments shared with loved ones and enemies. William was right: it was all in his distant past now. He had to try to forget it all and concentrate on the task at hand. That was, in this moment, to sweep the floors of the sleeping quarters which took up most of one floor of the ship.

Men were piled in together with little concern for their welfare and comfort. Some couldn't cope with the conditions and had been driven to madness or, at the very least, a sense of painful distraction from the present moment.

Elijah felt he would be one of them were it not for William and his sensible words, which caressed his ears and soothed his soul on many a desperate occasion. It was paramount to them both that they avoid the wrath of the ship's chain of command, brutal and scornful of the underlings as the crew's superiors were. Elijah and William made a promise to always be there for one another, if they could, the journey sealing what had been many years of immeasurable companionship.

"Elijah!" a voice called from the upper deck, and Elijah went immediately to investigate the concern. "Is this what you call sweeping?" the man said, recognised only as Peter, the barbaric ship mate who had driven many of his peers to the brink of suicide.

"I haven't started the upper decks yet. I am still doing the work you set for the sleeping quarters," Elijah countered, unaware of having done anything to warrant his name being shouted at full volume.

"Any slower and you'll be here at midnight. Now hurry up with your orders because I have more for you where those came from." Elijah scrambled to obey the domineering Peter, and quickened his pace downstairs to finish his work before ascending to the upper deck.

When he got there he found a group of men standing around discussing something seemingly important in hushed tones. Elijah could not help but listen as he began to clear the debris of the previous day's activities.

"We can't go on much longer, Paul. We'll start to starve soon or worse!"

"I know, I know. But we can't just kill him. There needs to be some alternative to such a rash decision, though I can't think of any at this point."

"What if we tie him up and force him to come to his senses?"

"Too risky. We could get punished. He'd know who we are and report us for mutiny."

The conclusion was to surrender to the chain of command for a few more days, hoping that during that time the slight dismissal of orders and the rejection of the military hierarchy would be enough to satiate the men's growing need for revenge at the way they were being treated.

Although Elijah did not share the desire to kill his superiors, he sympathised with the need to make some kind of stand against the conditions they were being subjected to. They had not seen another soul apart from the same familiar, dejected faces on board the ship for weeks and many of the men wondered whether they would live to tell the tale of their crossing of the Atlantic.

Elijah tried to pretend he hadn't heard this discussion, mentioning it only to William whose eyes bulged in surprise at the audacity of his fellow crew.

Chapter Fifteen

The deep blue and turquoise of the ocean grew increasingly disturbed. Spray, and the remnants of waves, scattered the ship's deck whilst men cowered beneath the surface world, uttering well-worn prayers for their own survival. Some of the men were sent above board in order to fix parts of the ship which were falling apart. They never came back. The waves gulped them down into the depths beneath as if their lives meant nothing to this hungry beast of a storm.

The bow creaked, the floorboards leaked and for a moment Elijah believed this was his final day on Earth. He grew reflective and wondered whether he would see his mother again all too soon or whether God had an alternative plan for his life. If this was how he was going to end at least he had William and a handful of good men by his side.

They huddled together for warmth. Elijah recognised the men who had been sent to the ship's top deck, but had now perished. They were the rebellious ones planning to overthrow the hierarchy of command and replace it with something more suitable to their outlooks.

Elijah found it ironic that the very commands the crew were reeling against were the ones which caused them to meet their end. Perhaps they wished now they had taken the more drastic actions their conversations suggested were options.

However, now those plans had been scuppered and those remaining thought better than to rock the boat any further. At present it twisted and jarred in the currents, the screaming winds terrifying all on board and making them believe in nothing if not the certainty of death itself.

The drowning men's bodies were not far from the ship, their limbs reaching for safety in an inevitable and futile manner. Soon their souls were far from this world and all its sufferings.

The absence of these individuals both calmed and distressed in equal measure: trouble indeed had found the troublemakers. Elijah wondered what had become of them. Would they forgive the commanders who had finally sent them to their deaths? Did they regret enacting orders which would ultimately cause them to perish? These questions could no longer be answered and Elijah tried not to dwell on them.

The deep sea seemed entirely drunk, in disarray. It roared and laughed at the crew's helplessness. It was nothing less than God's mercy which eventually saw them through according to Elijah's pious vision. As the hours stretched on the waves began to subside and the ship slowly steadied itself as the tortured currents eased. It was a brand new day; Elijah and William were glad to see it.

Chapter Sixteen

"William! William!"

Elijah was frantically searching the lengths and depths of the Victoria for his beloved companion, the co-instigator of this journey. Hunt though he might, he could not find his friend anywhere. He had asked his fellow crew if they had seen him, but they all shook their heads. "Does no one care whether a man lives or dies anymore?" Elijah wondered while continuing with his potentially gruesome task.

William had not been seen all morning and Elijah feared the worst. He finally found him curled up in a foetal position overlooking the back of the ship.

"William, what's wrong?" Elijah blurted out, thinking not of the truth that his eyes were showing him. When he received no answer he shouted the question in a repetitive fashion.

William finally replied with the dreaded truth. "I'm dying, Elijah!"

"No, William. You're not. We'll get the doctor. He can save you."

Rushing in his torment, Elijah found the ship's medical expert and took him to where William lay. The doctor grimaced and did not want to go closer for fear of infection.

"It could be any number of things: diet, disease, exhaustion…" The doctor trailed off.

William moaned and shook in his agony.

"You must have something to help him with, doctor? Can't you see he's in pain?"

"Of course, of course," Doctor Jeffries replied, and administered a small dose of liquid to William, who cried with gratitude, repeating the words "thank you" over and over until they lost all meaning.

Still, there was doubt about the long-term effects of the medicine and Elijah got the sense Doctor Jeffries was merely placating his patient.

"Can you not do more for him, doctor?" Elijah cried, at last realising the truth of the situation. The contemplations of an increasingly lonely life without his best friend flooded Elijah's mind.

The doctor recommended Elijah return William to his bed and nurse him through what could be a fever of some variety. The lack of understanding infuriated Elijah, who got the distinct impression that one fewer hungry mouth to feed would not bother those in the higher strata of the ship's command. He, nonetheless, carried out the doctor's orders and returned William to his quarters.

It took some time for William to reach his bed. Wailing and aching every step of the way, he tried his best not to collapse on the spot with the pain of having to stay alive to see another day. It seemed William had given up before he had even begun the fight for his health, and cursed his illness whenever he could spare a breath.

The night was long. Elijah stayed by his best friend's side and ignored his chores, which annoyed the other crew members beyond words. Elijah knew he would get in trouble, but couldn't help himself: he had to know his friend was going to be all right.

In the midst of the night William took a turn for the worse and Elijah feared he would never hear a word from him again, but William pulled him close and whispered as best he could.

100

"Elijah! You know I have always loved you like a brother. I may be dying, but I want you to live, my friend. I don't care if you have to take ten thousand lashes for the price of it, live as a free man. I pray to your God that you find what you're looking for, what you've always yearned to find, whatever that may be…"

He motioned as if he were about to continue, but his weakness overcame him suddenly and, with those words, he vacated this Earth. William died in a pool of sorrow and remorse at ever having dreamed of this journey, and Elijah wept bitterly at his friend's departure, wondering what would happen next on this seeming fool's errand.

It had been Elijah's dreaming that had led them here, and ultimately what had killed his best friend. He cursed the world for being so cruel as to leave him completely and utterly alone, without even a fool as a friend or a whore as a wife. Nobody, it seemed, could stay long by his cursed side.

William's last message to Elijah weighed heavy on his mind, and Elijah returned from his spell of words to face some of the very lashings his friend had spoken of. He received ten strokes in exchange for his lack of chores, and all the while Elijah dwelt upon the price of freedom.

Chapter Seventeen

Following William's departure from this world, the chasm which Elijah felt in his life was briefly filled by his fascination with an older man on board named Benjamin Brut. Ben was Elijah's senior by a full decade, their birthdays nearly colliding as they found out during the journey. There was nothing much to celebrate on either day. Yes, they were alive, but barely. Elijah dealt with his sorrow and pain by stealing some alcohol from the supplies, which were usually reserved for the higher ranking officials. He received yet more lashings when he was found, drunk and raging, below deck in a darkened corner of the sleeping quarters.

In his pain and confusion Elijah wept himself to sleep and awoke to find Ben offering him a hot drink. It was something akin to a dark night of the soul for Elijah, who had never felt more alone in his life. The long beard and straggly hair exhibited by Ben suggested a loss of vanity and self-care which Elijah related to wholly.

"How are you doing, young man?" Ben enquired, optimistically. There was no answer, fake or honest, but there was a slow stirring and a reach for the cup.

103

"That bad, eh? We've all been there."

At this Elijah recoiled and wanted to argue, but had not the energy or will for a confrontation. It was quite clear to Elijah that Ben's statement was incorrect: we had not "all been there", had not suffered the same, did not understand our own inner worlds, let alone those of others.

Most of the men on the ship were concerned merely for the continuation of their pulses, scraping and toiling their way through the days. Ben, however, seemed a more complex character, dismissive of his own mortality and curious about what lay beyond the veil between this world and the next.

"You know, Elijah, William was a good man. Young and naive, but graceful in his ways and caring towards those around him. I don't believe that death is the end. It's only the beginning of whatever lies ahead. William suffered in his last moments. Wouldn't you grant him reprise from his pain?"

Elijah stirred. "What about MY pain?"

"Well, that is just something you must learn to

live with, as we all do. Don't you think I've lost good men before? Don't you think good men lose their lives every day in this God-forsaken world? Every second on this planet has been filled with animalistic rape and murder since time immemorial. Don't you think there must be something more than this?"

Tears welled in Elijah's crumpled face once again. "I remember having a conversation with William about this. He said the same."

"There you go, don't you think a part of him will be relieved to know the secrets thus far denied us? No, death is not the end, but the beginning. The end of the beginning will be the beginning of another chance to get things right. I hate tomorrow as much as the next person, the struggles it will bring, the endless trying and the rare successes which taste different to the way they look. No, this world is not forever, but a blink of an eye and a flower in the wind."

Elijah admired the attempts to reach through to him, to offer him some comfort and ease his suffering. "You put on a brave face. Most of the men here live for tomorrow, hoping that somehow it will be better than today."

105

"Not I," Ben replied. "I find the entire human race to be simply one long prayer for something better. Still, you must believe as Christ rose again, so could you or I?"

"I don't believe as you do. I believe as my Grandmother once said: if you see beauty growing where now there is none, so it shall be in days yet to come. I live for the day when the world will be as beautiful to me as it was when I was a boy, carefree and happy."

"I believe you will see childhood again and again, which might not sound too appealing to you, but nevertheless it is the way things are in my eyes. This world is brutal and imperfect, yet we return to it in the same way a good man never leaves his wife and children, though they cry and want things from him he cannot provide."

"You really believe that?"

"Oh, and more. I have numerous beliefs, some of which are conflicting. No one knows the depths of what I hold to be true, least of all a stranger like you."

"Then why do you talk to me so nakedly?"

"Because you are suffering, and words are all I have."

"Then tell me more."

"What would you like to know?"

Elijah thought a moment. "If the world is so full of bad and terrible things, why would you want to come back?"

Ben sighed, and just as he was about to formulate an answer Elijah lost his patience. "You know, it makes no sense to me. William is gone and we will be soon, too. There's nothing more to me than flesh and bones. You too, despite your wandering convictions. Maybe there is something more, but only Christ understands it. Paradise is beyond the reach of most mortals."

"My convictions are not 'wandering' and have not been for some time. Listen to me, I speak words truer than memories! These are my deepest truths which I share with you now. Not many men would bother."

"Maybe you shouldn't."

107

Ben recoiled at this and whispered his words carefully. "And leave you alone as I have been? Although I've not wanted to be here for most of my adult life because of people's cruelty, shallowness, judgemental attitudes, malice, ignorance, selfishness, craziness, stupidity, evil, neglect and manipulation, I do occasionally glimpse the idea that it might be nice to try again."

Elijah had let him complete his lengthy list of negative attributes, yet with the impact of Ben's final words he finally conceded intellectual defeat. Whether he surrendered or was overwhelmed with logic seemed hardly a debate to be had, but he got up and dressed for the first time in days, washing and even whistling when the urge came to him. If William's soul had gone on to a better place perhaps he would watch over him as he tried his best to pursue his heart's desire, Elijah surmised. With the strength of two men, one in this world and one in the next, perhaps great things could be accomplished and his life wasn't over. Perhaps time was an ocean more endless than the one he was currently crossing.

Much as he struggled with Ben's words and

thoughts, thinking them somewhat crazy and ill-formed, he did take comfort in the way in which someone had at least made the effort to communicate with him in his darkest hour. The possibility of eternity shone to him once again.

Chapter Eighteen

The work never ended and Elijah found himself in a blur of days and months. He decided to bravely enquire with the ship's chain of command and find out the date. He knocked on the door of the officer's cabin and was reprimanded for his troubles.

"What do you want, boy?" came the bellowed reply from George, a shipmate with a fearsome reputation.

"I'm terribly sorry to bother you. I was just wondering what the date is."

"Haven't you got chores to do, boy?"

"Yes, sir. But I'm very keen to know the date before I continue with them."

The officer scowled at the younger man, but felt some inkling of pity for his desperation.

"It's February 2nd, 1727. Now be on your way before you get a flogging for insolence," George concluded.

"Yes, sir. Thank you."

As Elijah turned to leave George suddenly called him back. "Wait!" he yelled, confusing Elijah with his contradictory instructions. The officer then brandished something which brought yet more puzzlement to the inferior crew member.

"I believe this is for you," George clarified, and handed something to Elijah which the recipient took a moment to realise was a letter with his name on the front and an unbroken wax seal on the back.

"Thank you," Elijah offered and his good manners were met with a nod of approval from the officer.

Elijah's face showed no emotion, though deep down he felt many things. He scurried away from the officer's cabin and continued with his joyless tasks for the day, denying the urge to read his letter until a suitable opportunity to engage with its contents arose.

The next night Ben came with drinks that he had stolen. Elijah seemed disengaged, dejected and despairing.

Ben decided to get straight to the point.

"So tell me about your family. Your mother, your father?"

"Oh, I don't want to talk about it. You tell me about your mum and dad?" Elijah returned.

Ben sucked hard on the air that surrounded them and then exhaled a stream of words which shocked rather than comforted.

"Well, my mother committed suicide when I was a child. She hanged herself after spending a decade locked in a room struggling with the demons in her own mind. She was kept a secret from me for most of my formative years, worried as they were that her torment might be contagious. However, I still remember the odd, haunted days when I would meet her line of eye.

As I may have mentioned before this world chews people up and spits them out without a care for their souls: there must be a better place for her to dwell. Yes, I spent most of my life wondering where my mother was, how she was, who was caring for her. Now I will never know."

Elijah stopped and stared, not knowing where to look but in the irises of the eye of the storm. At last he formulated an answer for his companion:

"I'm so sorry to hear that. You must have been through so much to speak with such depth," Elijah deduced.

"The victory is mine because I'm still here," Ben spoke clearly and full of conviction.

"As for my mother, she was a seamstress, simple and plain. Her name was Jane Smith before marriage, then she became a member of the Keith family. It was a move she probably regretted in later life. Yet she fell in love and her fate was sealed. She knew nothing of the wider world and barely cared to. But she was good to her family, kind and fair, though she was bullied and pushed around by my father in ways that distorted her soul. I always felt there was a pain in her that I couldn't understand and then she was gone. Smallpox took her without showing the charity to take me too. I empathise with aspects of your tale and wish the best for you as you deal with the fallout from your past."

There was a pause in the conversation as information was digested by both parties. Once this had been accomplished Elijah continued on.

"It's my birthday today, that's why I'm feeling so down: there's no one to celebrate with me anymore. I just toil and scrub and the days pass, washing over me as though I was unconscious. But here I am, a year older and completely alone."

"Ah, my birthday blessings to you, young man! You know, it's my birthday in two days' time. I am here to celebrate with you. How old are you now? 23?"

"24," Elijah confirmed.

"You are brave to talk about it all while still so young - it took me years to be open with people about my family life! Here, let's toast to our ageing and move on with our lives. We can talk about your father when the moment comes. Cheers!"

They raised two glasses to their survival and put the rest to bed.

"So how do you feel now?" Ben said without a smile.

"Right on the edge of madness. How do you feel now?"

"Astonished by your bravery. I feel like I've known you all my life, as though I fundamentally understand the goodness of your soul."

"Thank you. I feel likewise, though I know not the answers to all of your questions."

"So, do you want to talk about your father now?"

Elijah braced himself before replying.

Knowing not the current condition of his familial patriarch he racked his brains for something positive to say, but found nothing.

"My father was a scoundrel. Often William and I," Elijah gulped thirstily on his drink, "used to wonder if he was saved. I never really knew my father. He seemed in his own way tortured beyond repair; his touch at times was weak rather than gentle. At others it was cruel as opposed to firm. I know I am lucky that he is still with us now, but I wonder if he'd recognise me sometimes. Tell me about your father."

Ben's answer came with more ease: "I knew my father before I began these sorrowful journeys. He was a good man, fair and honest. Taught me how to survive without him from an early age. Then I grew up, yearning for the big seas. So here I am. This is the edge of life and death, my friend - don't look down."

"But don't you sometimes want to die?" Elijah confessed his sadness at last.

"Don't you sometimes want to LIVE?" came the optimistic response from his confidant.

Elijah thought a moment, contemplating the battles of his inner world, the victors and losers of his great wars for spiritual, mental and physical survival. Finally he reached his conclusion: "Yes, I do. And, in all honesty, I think your mother made a mistake she can't ever undo."

"That's exactly how I feel, Elijah" Ben said with true affection in his voice. "Yet still, from love we are born, to horror we succumb." Ben seemed pleased by the wisdom of his own words, but they struck no chord in Elijah, who was busy contemplating the notion of suicide.

Elijah didn't believe in such unnatural endings and couldn't imagine the consequences of losing someone so close in such a gruesome manner. Indeed, his will to live may have fluctuated in recent days, but he held on to life with all the strength he could summon.

Chapter Nineteen

Over the coming days Ben's words and visits seemed to energise Elijah. They became embroiled in discussions during the evenings when the workload eased and the potential for intellectual enlightenment emerged.

It became clear that they were both educated men on a ship of predominantly less fortunate souls, and Ben boasted that he had even read The Bible's words for himself, confused though that had made him on many occasions.

"What I don't understand, older and knowledgeable though in some ways I may be, is how the Church has betrayed its calling."

Elijah, with his religious convictions and earnest intentions, balked at these words and, though he had come to respect their speaker in so many ways, could not accept this theory.

"It's true, Elijah!" Ben exclaimed at the sight of Elijah's disgruntled face. "The Bible says that a rich man going to Heaven is as likely as a camel fitting through the eye of a needle, yet when one looks at the wealth acquired by the Church one might think of these words as fiction. If a rich man going to Heaven is like a camel fitting through the eye of a needle, a rich Church doing God's work is something even more ludicrous. The wealth of religious institutions is a stain on humanity's conscience, laughter in the face of God. Material wealth and holiness are not compatible. At least, not according to the holy texts."

Elijah recoiled. "Every man on this ship wants to be wealthy..."

He was interrupted. "And few men on this ship desire to truly know God. Hence the whole world seems to have life backwards. You, I see, might be an exception."

"I am not a great man, Ben, no matter what you may see in me. I am a very average man with predictable limitations. I am not a profound philosopher or artist. I am an admirer and not a creator of brilliant work."

"You'd better hope so. Philosophers, artists, great minds. They create works which, at best, seem divinely inspired. Yet the creators themselves often live tragically and die young, surrounded by those who never understood them. I pray this is not your fate – or mine."

Ben seemed troubled, aware of the danger that existence brings.

Elijah replied with conviction: "I will live for today, knowing that tomorrow may be beyond my grasp. And why talk of Heaven when you also talk of coming again? Surely if you have read the holy texts then you will know only Christ has come again, that was his mastery. You do confuse me so."

Ben sensed an intellectual challenge and rose to it. "Ah, but Christ himself said all this and more shall his followers do. You must aim for the stars, Elijah. Who knows how far you will go, maybe they will talk to you one day."

"Don't talk to me about the stars," Elijah retorted. "I blame them for everything. They have looked down upon us since the origins of all problems. Look at us now! Still they do nothing."

The senior man countered this point by leaning on the wisdom of a literary great. "Ah, but as Shakespeare said: 'The fault, dear Brutus, is not in the stars, but in ourselves.'"

"Yes, but stars don't talk, Ben. And your beliefs are as confusing as your behaviour. Why do you come to me every day with your nonsense?"

Elijah had lost the thread of Ben's previously comforting communication; the links between utterances had become ragged and ill-formed. Ben was disturbed by Elijah's seeming cruelty, yet he was adept at muting confrontations.

"Because I want you to know that even in your darkest hour you are loved beyond words. I may not have all the answers, and the answers I do have may be nonsense to you, but in asking the questions you have come further than most of the men I have met in my life. Men more concerned with subjection and quarrelling rather than peace and love. Men who don't understand the urge to know more than their allotted portion of truth. Men who would rather die or kill than find out why they are here. Yes, it is a confusing world, and I seek not to add to your woes. I will leave you be."

With that the nightly visits stopped, and Elijah consigned the words Ben had spoken to the back of his mind, concentrating instead on the pressing issue of survival. He was alone again, more confused than ever, and wishing for a place to call home.

Chapter Twenty

Elijah was in a dreamworld, carrying out his day-to-day tasks as though he was a puppet pulled by strings with an unknown hand attached to them, when he heard shouting from the top deck. Primal and bellowing they came, these shrieks and wails of desperate men. He put his tools down and investigated the source of the commotion.

There he found a most arresting sight: Ben, shirt stripped and muscles bare, receiving lashes which cut the skin and seared the onlookers' minds.

"What has he done?" Elijah enquired to the man nearest him, a creature he had only known as David from Norwich.

"He was caught stealing alcohol from the Captain's supplies. The Captain wants him dead, I swear it."

The bubbling brook of blood on the sailor's back had seeped down to his remaining clothes, simple trousers and underwear which would now be stained forevermore.

The agony on Ben's face came from many sources. Primarily the pain of the lashes, but also simply the distress of still being here to receive them. Since his friendship with Elijah had collapsed, Ben took it upon himself to steal increasingly copious amounts of resources to quench his growing thirst. This time he had been caught, and seeing as stock had been going missing for weeks, the punishment was all his to bear.

Elijah watched for a few moments longer, taking every physical hardship on board as if it were his own, until finally he could take no more of the scene.

"Stop! It was me, I stole the wine!"

"It wasn't only wine that was missing, though. Stand back before you get hurt, lad!"

"No, it was me! I've been stealing for weeks! Leave this man be, you have your culprit!"

Never one to turn down an act of cruelty, the Captain, intimidating and tall, thought for a moment. It was an act of insolence, a confrontational deed of aggression, which could not be allowed to pass without regard.

"Have him tied up as well. Fifty lashes!"

The sailors stood shocked for a moment.

"GO!" Captain Drake bellowed, and the men followed suit.

The eyes of the two men met as they received their respective punishments and Elijah was glad that he hadn't left his companion alone in his suffering. He had not been alone in his, so how would it have been fair to allow the brutality shown to his only friend to continue unaccompanied?

The muscular men completed their gruesome task and the two more lean and broken men were returned to unfurl on their beds as far from one another as the Sun and the Moon, united in a shared agony.

Chapter Twenty One

Bruised, his flesh torn, and with fresh brutal memories to try his love for life, Elijah recuperated given some time. It was no easy task: bandages had to be changed, bloody mattresses re-used and nightmares were contended with. Even sleep seemed an ally no more.

Lying awake a few nights later, Elijah attempted to write in his journal all of the recent events. However, he did not seem capable of the task. Instead he lay awake and dwelt upon his life back home, all the chaos and certainty of it.

It was then that he remembered the letter. Elijah suddenly felt he had the time and inclination to digest it at that point. He removed it from under his bed and in breaking the seal felt himself to be venturing into a territory which could either harm or reassure, though he had no control over which emotions were to be conjured by the unknown words.

"Dear Elijah,

I wanted to apologise for the person I was or became during your younger years. I realise

126

now that you are a grown man my time for redemption may have passed, but I want to at least try to make amends before you leave your home forever."

It was a letter from his father which went on to explain at length how and why he had become who he had emerged as during Elijah's formative years. Elijah felt moved and read feverishly the excuses and elucidations that his father presented as the sources of his woeful conduct towards his loved ones.

Elijah was stirred and at many opportunities released his emotions through the act of crying. He cried for the years he had lost to anxiety and worry about what his father would do or say next, he cried with relief that at least someone else's suffering had been heard and contemplated by his paternal caregiver, he cried tears of forgiveness, anger and pain.

By the time he reached the end of the letter he was all but ready to return home and reignite his relationship with someone he thought would always remain estranged from him, but when he reached the final passage all this changed.

"Having children when I was still a child myself in many ways, not knowing how to behave or who to turn to, was..."

The concluding couple of words were scrawled in such a way that Elijah found them almost illegible, especially through his veil of tears. His bloodshot eyes and agile mind strained with effort. Did they - could they - say "a mistake"? It seemed as though the shapes of the letters suggested this to be the case, but Elijah's heart broke to contemplate the thought.

At this epiphany Elijah the letter tumbled from his hands and he felt the familiar senses of isolation and rage which had kept him a prisoner during his youth. He resolved to burn the letter and never think of his father again, a promise he kept to himself until his dying day.

To distract himself from the bitter disappointment of his father's words Elijah decided then to draw a picture of the land he was going to. It was better to focus on the future rather than the past in such moments, he concluded, brushing the residues of his visceral reactions to one side.

He picked up his implements and started to trace the lines and shadows of a beach, a jungle and then, finally, a mountain. It was all he could do to try to stay alive to see such places of wonder.

"Whatcha doing?" came a voice through the dark, stirring Elijah from his contemplations.

"Nothing," Elijah replied, and placed the diary next to his bed before blowing out the candle.

"Best not be trying to be too clever. You know what happens to clever folks out here," the unknown voice responded.

Out of curiosity Elijah looked in the direction of the speaker and, despite the dark, could make out the features of a man he knew as Stephen, the pauper who was kidnapped from Southampton's drinking regions and transported against his will to a destination not of his choosing.

All Stephen knew was that one minute he'd been drinking away his sorrows near the docks of his hometown and the next he was headed towards the edge of the world with no way back. No wonder he had a bone to pick with people,

Elijah contemplated. Regardless of the extent of a person's intellectual aims, there were always perils awaiting them. Yet Elijah was in no mood to be set upon.

He jumped out of his bed. "Look, what do you want from me? To slave and suffer all day and not express myself AT ALL? I was writing! Maybe if you could, you would too!"

At this, Stephen replied to violence with violence, following his primal instincts and defending his pride he sprang like a cat onto Elijah. They sprawled and battered one another until the man on watch, John, came and separated them.

"Now, now! No more or this or you're both in serious trouble. Do you hear me?"

The men had calmed down and eventually sleep was achieved by some, although Elijah only managed it in fits and starts. After this point he promised himself to keep his humble backpack on him at all times carrying his diary in, a secret he would keep from the world and a treasure purely for his own eyes.

Chapter Twenty Two

That night Elijah tried hard to put the pieces of his life together to make a pretty picture, but all he found were mistakes made, promises broken and disappointment after disappointment jostling competitively for prominence in his mind's eye.

He wrote in his diary of the need to belong.

"If you personally break through to higher plains, or however you want to phrase it, you'll still be dealing with the same raw materials that have seen every great teacher killed: ignorance, fear of the unknown, doubt, confusion and a jealous disposition towards the intelligent.

This fear of being isolated results in a huddling of people in the middle ground of not-knowing; people never asking the real, deep questions for fear of their answers; those who are disinclined to move towards the light of understanding for fear of getting burnt.

And I don't blame them. Having a natural desire to explore the outer reaches of my own mind, heart and soul, I have found there a madness I am scared to call my own as well as the extreme, blinding clarity of love itself."

After some contemplation he concluded:

"We all know precisely nothing. How wide is the world? No one knows. Therefore, do not think of yourself as being rich or poor in knowledge, for we are all beggars in the eyes of the Lord.

One man may think himself rich with a few coins, another may think himself poor with a small fortune. Yet God, who presided over the invention of money, laughs at the fools who parade their riches and feels pity for those who believe they never have enough. The contents of a good heart is the currency which activates the most powerful mechanisms in all the universe, it will move mountains and part seas, for all to see that the spiritual realm will never a bank be."

He thought of his beloved mother and how proud she would have been to see him live his dream. Sometimes he felt himself to be living just for her. He thought of all the times they'd helped each other in the day-to-day tasks of life and how he needed her to help him now, to give him the strength to go on. He prayed in his mind to her regularly and would do so in earnest again that night, tears hovering on the edges of his eyelashes, hope running through his soul like a visceral energetic force.

His prayer was an earnest desire for connection, to be heard, to talk to the great creator and really try to make contact with his deeper self. Why was he here? What is the purpose of all this pain and loneliness, one person after another leaving our sides until we, ourselves, depart this realm? To whom shall we answer for the errors in our ways?

He concluded his diary entry for the day, though he was unsure anymore of the precise date or place in which it was written. "Of all the great treasures scattered throughout the world is there no glimmer for me? I want just to hold, admire and love You, yet You seem somehow distant, unheeding or resistant. Show me behind the veil, to the true meaning of life. This is why I've come on this journey. To find You."

At that he went into a deep sleep and didn't return to consciousness for twelve hours. Apparently the men had tried to wake him, but he had remained asleep. Grateful for the rest - really, to what did he owe this honour? - he began to dress and then joined the men

133

upstairs.

He found, to his horror, another flogging.

This time the man wasn't close to him, but the anxiety of watching someone so in pain overwhelmed him. Suddenly he went to the side of the boat and threw up what little was in his stomach over the side of the ship. Retching was a harrowing experience for Elijah and he loathed every second of his existence for half a minute. This experience, such abject hatred of life, shocked him. He knew he would remember the extremity of his feelings for many years to come.

Alone and completely rudderless as a human being with only his prayer to guide him, he began to think of others' suffering to help him through. For he was not alone in his confusion. There was plenty of evidence of trauma and strife everywhere he looked: the scars on the men's arms and faces, the missing teeth and easily frayed emotions; all screamed of a dog that had been mistreated and now had a temper.

This sense of aggression was being poured around the ship, Elijah observed, until one day it overflowed.

Elijah awoke one morning to hear a cacophony of cries coming from the upper deck. In investigating he found streams of people coming from the Captain's office and followed them to their source. There lay the murdered corpse of the Captain, cheers and outrage intermingling in response to the scene. It was initially unclear who the culprit was – perhaps the bloody act had been carried out secretly during the night – but Captain Drake's murder left a chasm of command which proved hard to fill.

A long queue formed for the position of head of command, but no one won the dreadful competition. Instead small groups of men formed. One, around the suspected murderer, Matthew, was particularly feared, but seemed to lack the manpower to dominate the whole group - disparate forces popped up wherever they looked, it seemed.

Finally, all the men began working together after realising that if they did not they would surely perish. One needed the other like the sea and the land, merely for its own existence.

Chapter Twenty Three

The movements of the sea seemed to bother Elijah more than usual; the highs and the lows mimicking his inner world. Disorientating and endlessly in violent motion, they left him consciously trying to find calm.

He dwelt on the gratitude he felt at times to be alive when so many now hadn't made the journey. Among the illness and the sickness he recognised a few friendly faces, but couldn't bring himself to treasure them intimately. He felt as though his heart was full.

Elijah thought of William often. He fashioned a small cross, the symbol of Christ, in order to make an intimate shrine for his friend. Among his prayers were wishes for his deceased companion's safe arrival in the afterlife. He knew William wasn't a believer and Elijah didn't deem himself worthy of instructing the great creator and His Son, but he prayed William had found his way to the light.

His mother was a more difficult prospect to pray for: every time Elijah thought of her face the smell of her came back to him. It tormented him for days sometimes, returning to haunt him at times of anxiety, a familiar mixture of cleanliness and safety, though now he found none.

In spite of the fact that he had prayed at times for his father before reading his letter, Elijah's emotions towards him had always been confused. Though his father had explained he was now a free man, where would he go now? Into the arms of a new lover? Would he return to prison again soon, despite his claims to be a changed man? For what should he pray? A new soul, good and secure? A new personality, tolerant and respectful? The task seemed overwhelming to Elijah and he now prayed for his father no more.

For his brother, Thomas, he wished for him to create the stability their own childhood lacked. He prayed that the stories Tom had been given about life could be written anew, that the great waves that sometimes abound in a family will not drown him.

For his own journey he asked simply to be guided on the right path, speak with God and know the truth of life. No small aims for a young mind, but his ambition had taken him this far and he had faith in the existence of a future beyond the bows of the Victoria.

PART TWO:
The New World

A Moment Of Perfection

Chapter One

The sight of land, the slim crescent of a beach, brought cries of exultation from many of the crew's lips. Unbeknownst to them they were much further south than they had originally intended, but it was indeed the New World Elijah had been promised. Those who were left standing had endured a barrage of strife ever since leaving their homes; many thought that they would never live to see this blessed day. Soon they walked upon golden beaches, falling and kissing the sand here and there, whooping with joy.

Landing in the New World was the first moment Elijah had felt truly happy since he departed England, and he tried to imagine he was seeing it on William's behalf, as well. He savoured the sensations, the tingles of pride and the lightness of his being. Elijah even caught a glimpse of his emotions echoed in the faces of his peers; it seemed all around there was a newfound sense of wonder.

Everything about the New World shone: the sea glimmered with calm perfection and the sand seemed a glowing golden colour Elijah had never before known. Mostly he was aware of the distinct lack of anything resembling a cloud; Elijah was startled by the juxtaposition with the roughness of the world but a few miles away from such a utopia.

When the anchor had gone down and the crew descended onto smaller boats the jubilation in the air mutated into a mild sense of panic about the next stage of their journey. Elijah and the rest of the crew were always on the lookout for foreign creatures lurking in the trees and shrubbery nearby, but so far it would appear that they were alone and far from safety.

They settled down for the night, tents and equipment evacuated from storage units dotted around the ship. The stars looked down upon them as they slept uneasily, the sky a seeming altar to the divine forces that had led them here. Elijah found himself clinging to his company for hints of how to act and what to do. He knew nothing of the correct procedure at such times and relied heavily on his makeshift chain of command in order to structure his day and movements.

As the sun rose the clarity of Elijah's vision returned to him. It was just like the first picture he drew in his diary! In checking his sketches he found a similarity worth noting and he was breathless at the surreal synchronicities of life. After admiring the paradise he seemed to have found himself in he immediately investigated the foliage and delights that this new land offered.

At dawn there were search parties organised to investigate the surrounding area. Elijah found himself in a team of five: Gregory, Peter, Martin and Richard were his companions for this part of the journey. They each took it in turns to lead the group rummaging through unknown and inhospitable terrain.

There were constant screeches of birds and mammals they knew not the names of and cared little to investigate. They left that to the experts in the crew, who were busy making notes and keeping diaries of their every encounter. Elijah never told them of his own works, smattered with drawings and the key notes which he hoped would keep him alive and healthy as well as externalise his innermost wonderings.

As they made their way through the greenery, reunited with the sense of stillness only land can bring, the feelings of jubilation subsided and there was increasing curiosity and even wariness of their surroundings. Before they got too lost they would return to the ship for supplies and instructions.

Back at camp those who had inveigled their ways into positions of power and influence seemed pleased with the crew's progress, organising hunting parties to bring back anything edible with the intent and purpose of celebrating their newfound home.

On the third day the expeditions into the forests revealed access to a jungle, thick with the trees of ancient times. Upon the fourth day Elijah's group were given a very dangerous mission to venture deep into the foliage; they had looked at each other with disconcerted glances. Still, the instructions were followed and in the midst of the rush to leave Elijah forgot his diary. He returned to find it being read by a fellow shipmate and immediately snatched it from him and continued his business.

Elijah felt that the book was his only connection to home, the land which now was so far removed from his daily surroundings that any hint of it brought tears to his eyes. Lonely, and in some ways so very lost, he continued to search for a reason to be alive despite his contentment at having arrived in this new land at all.

It was the fifth day after their arrival when the troubles started. A search party had been attacked by natives. Not Spanish, Dutch or French, but local tribes with spears and hunting equipment which could be used for war. Several of the crew returned injured and two didn't return at all.

The crew began to wonder about their fates and brought increasingly aggressive supplies on their excursions into the jungle. Elijah began packing for battle instead of exploration and his shoulders became broad from carrying heavy chests from the boat to the shore. A new man was being born in the midst of the foreign features of this unknown land.

Elijah soon found himself moving among mud and swamps, in the sun and sweltering heat. It was a testing, trying time which he was determined to make it through once again.

Chapter Two

Deep in the midst of the jungle the tribe made its way through the day. The women cooked and cared for their young, the men hunted or smoked together in a deep trance. The young men trained for war and the old men kept the peace. Among it all there was an overwhelming sense of harmony.

For many moons the Shaman had been worried; afraid of invaders, for the tribe, for the future. Today he would have a ceremony in order to ask for guidance.

Using his expert knowledge of the plants and substances of the jungle, he went into a deep trance quickly with little need for assistance. His calm face betrayed his pleasure at entering this unusual state of consciousness, in which everything flowed as clearly as the rivers which made their way through the land.

The Shaman patiently awaited the arrival of the images which would inform him of his future course of action. In this frame of mind he could see a mountain, holy in its awesome presence, a road to it and instructions to follow. He also saw a foreigner, bruised and confused, yet with a heart like a blazing sun, shining a piercing light onto all. He heard voices telling him of a special arrival, a young man from far over the seas. When the Shaman asked where the foreigner was from he was told England, though he had little knowledge of such a place.

The vision continued and a woman appeared. The Shaman thought he recognised her form and face, but could not see enough to identify her fully. Dancing together this Englishman and tribal woman were well suited and wondrous, sharing day and night between them evenly.

The Shaman awoke from the dream and, although groggy and stupefied, he knew he had to arrange for an arrival.

Chapter Three

Back at the beach an argument was reaching fever pitch.

"We should make camp here first, not venture out into the unknown. Who knows what we might find there? This is how sins begin: some people always think they know better." Simon, one of the outspoken members of the crew, was making his feelings known.

Elijah never really knew Simon so much as heard of him. His tales and exploits would live on after him, but Elijah took no notice.

"Shame on those who celebrate the progress of fools!" Simon had his final say before he stormed off into distant solitude.

Watching his shape moving against the skyline in the distance, Elijah's emotional world was uneasy: he had the distinct feeling that wisdom was being ignored, but knew not the right course of action to take in order to correct this situation. He spoke to the men about his concerns, but was met with an awkward silence in most cases and condemnation in others.

148

Elijah was clearly in no position to make a difference to proceedings.

The attack came at dawn. No one was prepared. Elijah woke to find men dying all around him as he struggled to find his weapons. But he was too late, the attack had finished almost as soon as it had begun and the enemy had fled once the crew had awoken en masse to confront them.

Among the corpses Elijah saw Matthew, the crew member supposedly responsible for the murder of Captain Drake, who had become somewhat of a pivotal figure among the group. Although it was his first sight of battle, Elijah was ambivalent when looking upon the murdered suspected murderer and he turned away to search out more familiar faces.

It was then that Elijah found a sight to pierce his already-broken heart: Ben, his lifeless body swimming in a pool of his own blood. The face of the deceased looked remarkably peaceful, Elijah noted, but he could not reciprocate such placid emotions.

It was while taking in the gory scene that Ben's words echoed through him: "From love we are

149

born, to horror we succumb." He heard the speech of his friend deep within his soul. Finally, Elijah understood his friend's insight now that it was too late to give him the credit he deserved.

In a state of inner chaos and desperate for vengeance, Elijah ran towards the forests and fought back leaves and branches in place of men, venturing deep into the jungle with no instructions to do so. He became quiet and listened for sounds of enemy activity. He thought he had lost his mind, but then to his right he heard the rustling of movement, and followed it to a place of danger and intrigue.

He found nothing except birds and rodents, crawling and seething around the floor and sky. He realised he was far from safety and swung around to return to the ship. That's when his consciousness ended and after a sharp pain in his arm he fell to the floor to join the spiders and insects in their quest for space.

He awoke slowly, realising immediately that something was wrong. There were strange voices all around him and when he opened his eyes he saw nothing except the bare flesh and fire pits of the enemy. He panicked and reached for his knife, his gun, his shield, his diary, his clothes – anything familiar. He found nothing. Only his own near nakedness and the sense of drowsiness that comes from being poisoned.

Upon realising that their captive had awoken the men and women around him stirred into action. Strange words were spoken and fresh, cooling water was applied to the forehead of the ailing patient.

"What do you want from me?" Elijah braved the question in Spanish.

Immediately someone who recognised the words burst into the hut. Dressed in his primal tribal uniform and with a battle-scarred face, he mumbled something incomprehensible and told the others to leave.

"Where are you from?" the Spaniard bellowed.

Elijah did not want to answer for fear of his life.

"Don't worry, we won't hurt you. Just tell us where you are from."

"England," Elijah obliged. With that the Spaniard's face dropped and he soon left the tent to no doubt relay this information to his companions.

Elijah had no idea what to do. With all of his newfound strength and the will of God on his side, he could still not overcome these people; even if he could he had no idea how to get back to the ship and no seeming will to do so. He lay back down and prayed for salvation one more time, begged for a way out of this mess and all of the spiders' webs in which he now found himself. It felt hopeless.

It was dark outside and from the entrance to the hut – which was guarded by an imposing older man of about 35 – everything for miles around was faintly illuminated only by moonlight. The familiar celestial body which had followed him to the other side of the globe was the only other light besides the fire which these strange people had lit, showing their markings and scars in a dim and terrifying glow.

Chapter Four

Elijah spent several days in the hut, being fed and watered by exotic women who initially flinched at his accidental touches. As the days passed, presumably, his stench had become unbearable: one of the women of the tribe was assigned the duty of ensuring he washed.

Adelita had a soft, feather-light, gentle soul with passion like a wild fire. She had the brownest skin he had ever seen, a night without the stars. However, she sparkled to Elijah. Feelings stirred in his being which felt alien, for he hadn't felt them for some years, if at all.

Something about her lingering touch let him know that she didn't find him repulsive.

"What's your name?" he asked, naively in English. She smiled and the fields of paradise were in full bloom.

Elijah quickly finished and returned to his hut, fully aware that something had happened, something ineffable. A dance had begun, the slow swaying of emotions taking them both by surprise.

The next day he saw her as he was led from one small holding to another. She herself bathed this time, covering no body part from prying eyes in shame. Indeed, she seemed to have none.

On the third day she came to him, that same smile on her face. After she had sneaked past the sleeping guard he could hardly believe it as she sat down next to him and touched his knee. At Elijah's flinch, she turned and said to him in perfect Spanish:

"Has nobody ever shown you how to express your affection before?"

Startled, Elijah felt his masculinity to be at stake. All his religious convictions could not hold him back from this act: indeed, perhaps his love for God and life fuelled his embarkation on this new and enticing quest for connection. He made love ferociously, like an untamed animal.

Chapter Five

Elijah awoke alone again and was finally summoned by the Spaniard and taken to a much bigger, more impressive holding in which a small crowd of natives had gathered. There were plants and artifacts all around which Elijah could not identify and he became afraid once again of what the future held. He finally came face-to-face with the figure who seemed to be a medicine man or key member of the tribe, according to Elijah's ignorant assumptions.

The Englishman felt small and full of anxiety, especially after the strange dream of the night before. He had heard that natives would eat foreign travellers and put their heads on sticks as a warning for their enemies to see.

"This is the (…)," the Spaniard said to Elijah. The Englishman did not understand the last word of the sentence, the noun around which all meaning hung, and scrambled around for close equivalents. Not a medicine man, not a tribal elder. Finally, Elijah concluded that the word must be "Shaman" in English, the mother tongue which he now missed dearly. It was an obscure word, only found in the most peripheral books, but Elijah had heard it before.

"He has been waiting for you."

A knot tied itself in Elijah's troubled stomach, which for days had been fuelled on strange foods for which he had no name.

"I'm sorry, I do not understand. Where am I? Where is my crew?"

"Silence!" the Spaniard roared. "He has been waiting for you," he repeated calmly.

Elijah gave up trying to make sense of the situation and decided to make conversation as smooth as possible. "What does he want from me?" seemed to be the most sensible thing to ask at this point, and in reply he was greeted with several pairs of eyes glancing sideways at one another. The Shaman finally spoke.

A totally unfamiliar dialect filled the air and the Spaniard translated for Elijah so that he might understand.

"The Shaman has had a vision."

Silence prevailed among the others as the Spaniard spoke these words.

"A man from a foreign land would come and bring knowledge to his people, travelling across the rough seas and speaking of the future. He believes you are this man. Now we would like to hear the words which the Shaman has longed to hear. We have healed you…"

Elijah interrupted: "You have attacked me and kept me prisoner…"

"Only for your own good," the Spaniard continued, unamused at the interruption. "You were moving into lands which are not safe for your kind."

"What happened to the other men?"

"They are with the spirits. You should have no further concern for them."

Elijah wondered if this was true, and felt a strange sensation of dread come over him when thinking of what life would be like from now on.

"What do you want from me?" he squealed, grabbing at his hair and creasing his face, unashamed of his naked fear.

The Shaman understood and reached beside him to show Elijah a piece of paper which was damaged and worn. Elijah did not know how this would answer his question and began to beg to leave, at which point he was silenced by the tap of a spear on his shoulder.

"This is a map to a sacred mountain. If you follow it you will understand why we have saved you. You must travel there and return to us with knowledge from the top of the mountain about our future. There are many strange people from foreign lands arriving at this time. You are to tell us what the future holds, for we ourselves are uncertain."

With that Elijah was handed the map and given some men to accompany him out of the jungle. The first tribal man to be sent with Elijah was Matzika, a fearsomely towering man strong enough to fell a gorilla with his best punch. Beside him stood Mazula, ready for service. As the older man, Mazula was a coiled spring of insight and knowledge. His incessant muttering had Elijah on edge at times, but his eyes would penetrate the deepest foliage to find knowledge of its contents.

Elijah wondered whether he could return to the boat, but then realised that all had been lost in that regard and, faced with little choice, he followed the tribesmen to the end of the forest and kept walking alone.

"Don't forget, Adelita is waiting for you!" were the last words spoken by Matzika - with a cheeky grin - before Elijah wandered out of sight. Elijah promised to return to these people and bring knowledge from the mountain, but the reality of being alone in unventured territory overwhelmed him.

The Shaman had even shown him some real magic as he left: he had returned to him his backpack with the diary in it. Furthermore, when he looked back at the hut as he went to leave he realised that it looked exactly like the second drawing he had made in his precious book. He pulled it out, held it up and marvelled at God's work!

Then he had the realisation that the mountain would be the third image on his journey. He felt then that he was on the right path to find whatever it was he was looking for.

Chapter Six

The road was long. It stretched for miles in both directions from one horizon to the other. With the sun bearing down Elijah could feel the presence of vultures in hidden corners. Shadows made him jump. His tiredness bore down upon him like a cross, his desires were lashes across his bare back. Yet on he marched, clutching his last flask of water.

Circles were his only company; the movements of the celestial bodies above him, the curve of the Earth beneath him; the orbits of his changing patterns of thought. Once, twice, ten times he would view them, the moments which had seemingly disappeared without trace and yet now would come back to haunt him. His footsteps became heavy and often he stumbled and fell. Eventually he grew weary of picking himself back up again: with no company and no hope, he lay down to take his last breath.

He awoke in a medical tent, knowing not the wider scene of which it was a part, blind to the details of his circumstances and destiny. His eyelids flickered and then burst open. "Where am I? How did I get here?" He thought the words he could not speak and scanned the room. He was not alone anymore. The doctor who consumed his gaze was looking intensely at his notes and had not noticed his patient's stirrings. Upon this realisation the medical professional called for assistance and in walked a bustle of people, all relative strangers to one another as well as to their distressed patient.

As Elijah tried to speak, he realised he could not summon the strength and began to drift back into the sleepy state of semi-consciousness in which he arrived. He awoke again to find his tent empty.

Meanwhile, the medical professionals huddled in sanitised corridors and discussed in Spanish this strange new arrival. "He was found by the roadside completely deranged, mumbling something in English about a mountain."

"He's miles from the mountain. He had no chance. It's lucky he was found when he was: I don't think he would have lasted much longer out there."

After a few days Elijah was moved to a different tent. He couldn't wait to be free and well again, but while he watched the hours pass he amused himself by conversing with the other patients in Spanish.

"Have you heard about the mountain?" Elijah enquired.

"The mountain's a dream. Give it up."

"I don't think so," Elijah retorted.

"Have you ever seen it?"

"No, but I have the directions to it."

"Then why are you here?"

"Because they're too hard to follow!"

Still Elijah was determined to try again as soon as he physically could.

"You should be careful, I've heard them debating whether or not to treat you alongside the mad ones. Any more of your ramblings about mountains and that's where you'll belong. No, it won't be long until a brighter day dawns for you and you will forget all about your futile quest. Where was it you were from again?"

"London."

☐"And what are you doing here? Is that all you're doing? Looking for this mountain?"

"Yes, why?"

"Just thought you might have someone or something else on your mind, that's all."

"I have lots on my mind, thank you." Elijah knew his company wouldn't understand. The fellow patients often looked at him in puzzled bemusement; this stranger in what was to them a familiar land.

"Have you ever tried to climb it?" Elijah asked a fellow patient, Pablo, one day. Pablo was an elderly man, frail and weak from living. He had little patience with those who pursued their dreams, seeing life as more likely to be a nightmare. A sneer was the only response to Elijah's querying until finally a briefly considered barrage of hate came forth from the man's dribbling mouth.

"I wouldn't dream of climbing that mountain o' yours. It's nothing but a delusion in the mind of the lost. I suggest you get yourself a real hobby.

Have you tried fishing?"

"Yes, I have tried fishing, but you have not tried climbing the mountain. Why do you speak with such hatred about that which you don't understand?"

"I fear it is you who does not understand. Anyone who dreams of such things - and I have seen a few - is giving their life away in exchange for nothing. There's nothing on top of that mountain except a drink for a thirsty fool!"

At this the conversation drew to a dispiriting close. Elijah knew he was listening to the words of the ignorant and his audience recognised the schemes of a madman. It was an impasse.

That night Elijah went to sleep and awoke to find the same man crying. "What's wrong?" the Englishman uttered, trying not to reflect the man's blinkered, brutal atmosphere earlier in the day. A few hours had changed the dynamics of their relationship immeasurably and now Elijah found himself trying to crawl out of bed to comfort his acquaintance.

"No, don't do that. You'll get me in trouble if you hurt yourself," Pablo insisted.

"Well, how can I help you?"

"You can't: I'm dying," Pablo whimpered. "I'm so afraid," he stammered amidst a fresh flood of tears.

"I have seen enough death for one lifetime. I don't wish to see any more; I pray that you will live a long and happy life!" Elijah exclaimed.

"Your prayers mean nothing to me, stranger. There's nothing you, the doctors or even God can do to change my situation. I just find it hard to accept, especially during the night when I'm alone in the dark with my thoughts of what's to come. I think of all the fields I've yet to walk through, all the sunsets I could one day admire, all the people I could share my love with; it all seems such a waste! I only wish I was stronger…"

At this Elijah gave up on his quest to placate his audience. Obviously Pablo was suffering in ways that were unknown to Elijah. However, he prayed for him day and night, and by the time Elijah was well again Pablo remained to admire another sunset.

It was three days after this incident that Elijah was declared well and released into the outside world. He was given a collection of his belongings, but after checking every single pocket of every single item he could not find what he was looking for.

"Where is it?" Elijah asked the doctor who had handed him his possessions.

"Your belt?"

"The map!" he roared, losing himself for a moment in panic.

"This was all they gave me," the doctor responded. Elijah had immediately opened his diary to find the key pages torn out and the map missing.

"They? Who is this 'they'?"

"My superiors," came the slow, respectful response.

"I need to talk to them."

"I'm sorry, sir, that won't be possible."

With that Elijah found himself cast aside; alone, bewildered and somewhat furious. He could remember bits and pieces of the journey from memory and perhaps natural instinct, but the Shaman had told him not to give the directions to anyone else. Now Elijah had let down the man around which he now orientated his life despite the fact that his intentions had been good.

He took a tentative step or two, shuffled around the gathering of small tents and then marched onwards. The hospital was a part of a bustling town and he felt as though he was in a forest he needed to escape again. He had no possessions except a back pack filled with resources. He set out on foot to find the same road he had travelled before, determined to conquer it.

It was early evening by the time he reached it and he decided to travel at night to avoid the glare of the midday sun. A night of sleeplessness was the least of his worries as his demons constantly harassed him with thoughts like claws and memories like snarls.

The road was twice as long as he remembered, but by the morning he had reached the end.

The stones grew bigger, the landscape mutated and soon Elijah found himself in a rocky canyon which stretched high and wide.

He slept in the geographical crevasses and feasted on the food he had stolen from the hospital. After a lonesome few hours of rest and finding shapes in sporadic clouds he moved onwards, knowing first that every step brought him nearer to his mission's completion and secondly that without some comfort and supplies he would soon perish. Now that he had passed the desert causeway there would be no fellow wanderers to rescue him. He had been fortunate previously, but he had no intention of testing his luck for a second time.

The canyon soon gave way to the lush vegetation of the forest, just as the Shaman had said. The rivers and streams seemed ripe and overflowing with blessings. Elijah even caught fish in the river using a pocket knife and a makeshift net to allow him to consume their fleshy nourishment. He was a survivor of some experience at this point, but this quest was testing his skills to their limits.

Eventually he realised he hadn't seen or heard another human being for days. As he wandered through the thickening mass of plants and vegetation he began to have doubts that he would ever do so again. Death once again played constantly on his mind. He wondered if Pablo was still alive today or if the veil had now been lifted. He soon found himself standing inside a moment that overwhelmed him, looking behind him and all around him for clues about how to progress.

At one point he simply sat on the bug-ridden floor and cried the tears of the searching. He remembered his grandmother's old, frail hands; their wisdom and experience were yearned for in this strange, foreign landscape: he questioned what he had become, from what he was made, the substance of his very soul.

When he embarked on the journey to the New World he had been a boy in all but stature, yet circumstance had led him on an inner trail towards self-awareness and insight. He remembered the Shaman's eyes as the medicine man instructed him on this seemingly futile mission. Now again standing on the precipice of life and death, he looked inside his soul and found nothing but the remnants of the people he had been.

169

"No," he thought, "this will not do!" Elijah wanted so badly to make some memories which did not torment and frighten him. He hoped he was on the right pathway, his truest journey. He slept uneasily near the stream where boars' roars and birds' chirps kept him in an in-between state of consciousness, testing his ability to stay sane.

With the trees stretching overhead and his focus on the ground beneath him, lest his footing fail him, he didn't notice the looming, ominous mass of land appear on the horizon. The first time he noticed the mountain he squealed with delight, whooping and hollering as if struck by a lightning bolt of ecstasy. His pace quickened and he began navigating the early stages of his elevation.

Closer the colossal mass of earth and rock came, and his joy began to subside. A terrible sense of fear came over him: what if he died, what was he thinking, why did he feel so small? Questions clouded his mind about what it would be like to reach the top of this immense natural presence. Would the victory taste as sweet as his battle suggested it would?

He was waging war indeed, unseen, against human frailty and his own pessimistic aspects. In doubting his potential to defeat his foes his fears began to grow. Soon he was engulfed by thoughts of something going wrong at what he had presumed to be the final hurdle. The dangers of tomorrows overwhelmed him.

Chapter Seven

Adelita put down her container of water and steadied herself. She was feeling faint on repeated occasions and could not understand why. Swaying and weak, she rested against a wall in a seated position until her tribal superior came to find her.

"Where is the water, Adelita? I am wait-"

At the sight of Adelita's weary expression the woman, Soma, stopped her berating.

"What's wrong, Adelita?"

"I don't know. I don't feel well at all."

At this she was taken to a healing woman, Mana. The tribal elder was gentle but firm, and when she was finished with Adelita the younger woman got a nasty surprise. After an extensive examination and a great deal of questioning the healer concluded that Adelita was expecting a child.

The pregnancy came as a shock and she felt the crushing weight of expectation reduce her to dust. Adelita soon felt the nights grow longer and the days shorter as she spent the evenings laying awake thinking of her new journey in life. Of course, childbirth was natural. But she had never been through it before and she knew the dangers involved. Several women had come close to dying during the birth of their children, and some had even passed over.

Adelita prayed that this would not be her fate. Since Elijah had gone away she had felt somewhat alone in the village. Danger was always close and she could have used a strong young man to protect her. Feeling deluded as well as unwell, she decided that she had felt too much for this virtual stranger and returned him to the back of her mind.

She had done all she could: Adelita had begged the tribal leaders not to send him away, she had given herself to him when she had felt the strange pull of his closeness, and the winds of her desire had always blown strongly and freely in her experiences.

Now she contemplated a life potentially without her new lover, for who knew what would become of Elijah? He had been gone but a short while in the objective scheme of things, but no one knew if he would ever return. With or without her love, it would soon be a life of motherhood and new trials which she couldn't seem to fully foresee.

Chapter Eight

Elijah fell, his limbs twisting and jerking like a firework. He had not anticipated the looseness of a boulder which he was climbing and now plummeted to the ground below. Terror gripped him, desperate as he was for any possible end to his torment besides death itself. Grasping and grabbing at everything that came his way he finally managed to slow his descent to a halt just in time, but nothing worked anymore: his limbs were all distorted and sore. He finally fell unconscious.

When he awoke the stars above him were glowing and all seemed peaceful except the throbbing pain in every inch of his being. He tried to stand, but couldn't. He tried to walk, but failed. He desperately wanted to run.

This place of dreams and wonder had become a perilous nightmare. Finally he rolled himself over. He smiled in the face of misfortune and the stars twinkled back at him. Still, he had come so far. Bruised and tormented, he had to keep going. This was all a test of his spirit, one he had to pass or die trying to.

Elijah reached for the water he had gathered

175

from the stream and drunk almost all of it. He needed that water as much as he needed every breath he had ever taken and was thankful to the Earth for providing sustenance. Slowly, tentatively he sat up. But could he stand yet? No, was the answer as he stressed and strained.

Above him the stars held their penetrating gaze. As he couldn't stand upright he felt he had no option but to sit and watch them while recovering his strength. He began to make shapes out here and there, wishing all the while that he was an expert at such things. The mysteries of the universe were far beyond him. Was it a chaotic mess or was there some shape and form, a purpose even? He wondered for a while, in his pain, about the unanswerable questions of life: where do we come from? Why are we here? What do we do with all this agony?

Elijah decided to say a prayer. He bowed his head in deep reverence to the great forces that govern what is. Whether one called them energies, natural forces or Gods, we would all bow our heads one day, Elijah surmised.

So he prayed:

"Dear God,

If you could allow me to escape this situation

I promise to always have faith in you.

You have taken me this far:

You have walked with me, cried with me, sang
to me through the birds
and the trees.

Take me now to the apex of my understanding;

Do not fail me and leave me to perish.

Much as I yearn to know the sweetness of the
afterlife,

There is still work to do here.

Help me find within myself the courage to
persevere;

Source in me the indomitable strength of the
warriors of yesteryears.

Inspire me to take another step, though my

177

foothold may be loose.

Show me you are there for me through my nights and days;

Make it clear that you care for me in every conceivable way.

Let me be a servant to you for the rest of my days.

Should I make it out of here alive

I promise not to be shy to say your holy name,

Not to cower in fear when fools attack me from all sides.

Help me to conquer what I don't understand,

Piece by piece,

As you are the master of me.

I have heard of your mysterious ways,

Shown to pilgrims and Saints:

Now show me my way.

I will be singing your praises

Every day, in every way,

Until I, with your permission,

Sit loyally by Christ's throne.

Amen."

Elijah lifted his head as if from a sleep, a deep yearning for life filling his weary body. He looked up at the night sky, overflowing with perfection. He admired the shapes, mysterious or well-known, and as he did so a shooting star blazed a trail across the skyline.

The combination of the clear night sky and this celestial greeting seduced him wholly: he felt certain his prayer had been heard, that there had been an answer, some shred of recognition for his need for communication from external forces. In short, he felt he was not alone.

He hid his head again and thanked God for the interaction which had no doubt saved his life. As he rose he felt within him a super-human strength, a will to live and continue on his trail, which he had never before known himself to possess.

He stood shakily before brushing himself down and checking that nothing was broken. In his search for wounds he found his left arm didn't move in certain positions. He was damaged in ways visible and invisible, desperate to complete his mission and escape the tortures of his journeying days.

He yearned for solidity, stability and calm. Someone to rely on and call his own. After he had climbed this so-called sacred mountain – this epicentre of pain and isolation - he would give up his travelling and find a sweet girl to settle down with, he swore. Perhaps Adelita would keep him, he pondered. He certainly would cherish her and give anything to be with her once again. But there was something about this current mammoth task which could not be left unresolved.

Ever since he had heard the tale of all the others who had taken up this perilous task and failed he had considered it a challenge to his very soul to see what others hadn't.

Chapter Nine

The biting, cold wind had arrived and, babbling like a brook, Elijah began to talk to the celestial bodies. He spoke eloquently about his mother, his brother and his journey to his meeting with the stars themselves. All the while, in his mind, he held Christ in his suffering.

If Jesus himself had believed that God had forsaken him in his most painful moments, only to be proven mistaken, then maybe God was with Elijah's lowly self now. This thought buoyed him and he held his own in the fight against numberless demons for his own soul. "I don't have time to fear God. I'm too busy loving Him," he concluded in his monologue for redemption.

"Don't forget me, mother! I will come to you when the time is right," he spoke only in his mind, the discomfort of his every muscle becoming close to unbearable.

He thought regularly of Adelita and the moments they had shared. Elijah wondered where she was now. If she was naked and bathing, did she think of him also? It spurred him on to the point of primal passion for the moment and its lineage; time stretching out before him like tortured waves fuelled by emotions both low and high.

He could no longer distinguish between the good times and the bad; all became a cacophony of noise within his kind adventurer's soul. If only he could breathe one more breath he had a chance to touch the stars, he surmised, feeling like nothing else mattered.

Onwards he flew, a bird in the sun. Swooping here then soaring there. Solitude became his only friend once again. Often after a long, drawn out silence there would be a flurry of verbal acrobatics as Elijah tried to recall distant cousins, the address of his Aunt or the number of children in his classes at school.

Nightmares approached if he could not remember a child's name or a relative's birthday. He would berate himself for not being a better person. He just did not care enough for the people around him and what each of them had brought to his life: it was a moment worthy of keeping in a jar under the cupboard of his consciousness itself, a reminder to focus on the things in life which would remain important to him throughout his journey.

At times he thought he had gone insane. Sentences didn't always form properly and the wind became as silent as the reality of the stars themselves. Still all that surrounded his troubled being watched over him, provided for him, tested him. It also made him question his beliefs just for a second. Why was he on this journey? What did he expect to find?

At this his mind had finally won, and he sat down for a while to really think. What was he looking for? Christ Himself? Some sort of connection with life, nature and maybe even God, he concluded. Just a moment of clarity in which he was not lost in the confusion of his own mind, but could see clearly that which he was a part of.

The wind seemed louder now, howling almost, as he fumbled for his flask and downed its remaining contents. One more push to the summit or this would be the end of him.

Elijah awaited another shooting star, greedy for more miraculous signs. However, none came and he could only think that the one, solitary shooting star had become ever more precious as time went on, more remarkable in its isolation.

Instead he was plunged back to the mortal world and made his way down the slippery side of the mountain before re-joining the obscure path. There was more than one way up this natural colossus and he had options which, as he had found, were more or less perilous.

He hoped the path he had chosen would prove to be fortuitous.

"If only to find the right one," he wondered to himself amidst a collection of dreams and visions which constantly clouded his now chaotic mind. Was he going crazy? He had certainly been delirious at several points on the journey. Snarling and lashing at leaves in the jungle, crawling and begging on the desert road, screaming at the fish in the river when they escaped him.

Once he was poisoned by some fruit he ate from a strange and enticing tree. He was starving and logic suggested that if the fruit was good enough for the monkeys it was good enough for a human being. Unfortunately, logic was no guide in these realms and failed him on multiple occasions.

He had faced indigenous people, with their own Gods and customs, protectors of this most holy of places in so many ways. He had fits of confusion amidst the delirium of his memories, tick ticking from moment to moment as though it was a game of chess, returning to the same pieces again and again, rearranging his mind.

Now he approached the summit. His legs caving beneath him at times, his hunger ravishing, his mind clear and focused in this moment, he drove on. He kept going despite the piercing wind, the emptiness in his veins and the feeling that he had come too far into the unknown to ever turn back.

Chapter Ten

Having plundered his pleasant memories for all they were worth, Elijah found himself in a gloomy state of mind. His parents' separation, break ups with girlfriends; all this and more came to him, flooding his mind with abject horror. Yet all the mistakes of his life - all the blemishes on his soul - had not kept him from getting this far. And so he blundered onwards into the great unknown.

Elijah eventually approached a clearing. He clasped his hands in sheer bliss as the breeze blew against his form and the sun continued to slope towards the horizon. The air was crisp and sharp, though he had to drag hard on it to receive what he needed.

Such was his elation that he started to stumble like a blind man. Panicking at the thought of meeting his destiny face-to-face, he made little progress until he straightened himself and returned to his perilous task. His feet were hurting, his bones felt as though they were about to crumble and subside from the weight of his existential questing, yet he was here. He had made it.

As he approached the edge of the summit to have his most precious view of the world he recalled a simpler time. He had been eighteen years of age and he was staring intently into a solitary candle's flame. As he watched the blue turn to orange and yellow before evaporating into the night sky, he realised that whether we understood it or not there was a sense of perfection to all things, a process by which all must be governed. The rules of the universe were sensed, yet not understood; that did not mean they were not there. All there is was subject to nature itself.

As he stared out from the mountain top Elijah was enchanted by the beauty of it all: the desert lands of the east and the jungles of the west, the convoluted shapes of the jagged mountain range, the sun approaching the edge of the skyline as it prepared to set on another day. It started as a feeling, an inner sense, and then merged into something more profound; a deeper understanding that all had its place in the mortal tapestry.

He felt a peace he had never before experienced, a cessation of all concerns. As much as his limbs ached and complained about the perils of the journey, they were thankful in their own way to have reached its conclusion.

A calm surrounded him as he stood and watched the scene, breathed in the clear air and contemplated his surroundings. Yes, he was as far from home as he could possibly be, and yet he felt strangely at one with everything, the overwhelming sense of someone who had found what he had been looking for flooding his being.

His mind started to swirl with questions. What about all the bad experiences he had been through? What about all the moments in which he felt no one could understand him? What about all the lost and lonely people in the world, struggling to make their way through? Some fell down: Elijah had known those who had committed suicide in slow and more rapid manners, going down in blazes of hysterical sadness and confusion.

For a brief passage of time, Elijah could see none of that. He was glad to have had this wondrous experience even once in his precious life. He reached into his backpack and pulled out his diary, which contained a sketch done weeks before of the exact image he was now beholding.

He held it up to compare the drawing with the reality, and was struck by the similarities of form and shape. The mountain stood in all its glory, surrounded by every nuance of the natural world. He had often practised the act of appreciation, and did so again in his present experience. He had found exactly what he was looking for: a harmony almost not of this world. At this time everything seemed right; an emanating calm amidst the chaos: a moment of perfection.

Chapter Eleven

Far in the distance Elijah saw storm clouds gathering and wondered what the future held. It was at this point that, as though a spell had been cast by his thoughts. tiredness overwhelmed his aching limbs and he dropped to his knees in a fit of delirium. Like a madman, his mind was filled with profound answers to his questioning of the future, visions forming from a source he could not identify.

Again the change was initially slow, images flooding his consciousness from an unidentifiable source. These visions started to dominate his senses, the perception of order he had just touched upon now making its way into the background of his mind. Into the foreground came tumultuous, screaming depictions of life and glimpses of experiences he would much rather forget.

He saw the world as he knew it, his childhood, his pain at the loss of his family connections. But the vision grew more abstract, a raging beast of insight and foreboding: images of war and rape, the destruction of the Earth. He saw the white man, triumphant in his mission to dominate the world, caring not for his obligations as custodian and guardian of those less fortunate.

He dwelt upon the experiences of slaves and people without rights, trodden upon in the mission for progress. He beheld nations rising against each other, risking everything in order to move the lines on their maps just a few miles east or west. Women and children were lost in maelstroms of war and pain, rape used as a familiar weapon of conflict. And all around was the foul sense of a greed that cannot be quenched.

It wasn't just the rape of each other that alarmed Elijah, but of themselves and the world around them. Shifting from the human world to the animal kingdom, Elijah watched as dolphins became caught in nets too big to discriminate between fish and other passing sea creatures. Whales were harpooned by feckless hunters who gorged on the flesh of the innocents.

He saw thunderstorms, floods, droughts, earthquakes, volcanic eruptions and forests stripped for their provisions. He saw diseases, plagues and famines destroying the societies of all nations.

He saw children being brought up in war zones, too shocked to see the light. He saw families broken and contorted, people who barely knew their own name.

He saw people leaning on drugs in order to maintain their mask of contentment. He was shown people holding the carcasses of the holiest of creatures, death an honour to an animal and a tragedy for a white man. He saw people moving, moving but never settling. They were too afraid to make anywhere their home.

He caught glimpses of the rich living in palaces with a hundred empty rooms while the homeless struggled to survive on streets that were not filled with good Samaritans. He saw animals in cages yearning to be free. He watched as women were pressured incessantly to be younger and more beautiful as men were told to hide their feelings beneath a mask of violence.

He was shown pictures of a world in which mental health problems had become so prevalent no one knew anymore who was sane. He saw people awaiting a redeemer, a Saviour who never came. He was privy to the prayers of the faithful uttered deep in the night asking for a peace that could not be found.

Altogether it was a hellish depiction of the only world Elijah had ever known. He wanted to look away, but wherever he turned his physical body more premonitions found their way into his perceptions. He was scared of these images, he felt contaminated in witnessing such suffering and sought to escape from his understanding itself. The future seeming a shackle upon the ankle of a slave to existence: were we all merely distressed prisoners of time and space? There seemed to be no escape from what is and what would soon be.

Elijah wondered about the Garden of Eden, the fall of man which had been taught to him in schools: was this where it lead? Was evil to rule the world forevermore? Could the Devil win his battle against the forces of divine love and justice for all?

Religious formulations aside, it seemed to him overwhelmingly clear that it was the human heart in which all good and evil can be sourced: people's behavioural and attitudinal choices were echoed around the wider world into the animal kingdom and the forces of nature

193

themselves.

Nothing seemed familiar, yet everything seemed the same. There was an overwhelming sense that a tapestry had been woven through the ages featuring the stark colours of greed, violence and destruction.

Elijah began to feel a personal sense of responsibility for this future, being himself a white man. After all, for what reason had he come on this journey? Financial riches? Wealth of experience and knowledge? Though he did not feel alike to the others, they were all on the same pathway.

Whatever the root cause of his dreaming it had ultimately led him to the truth. It was uncomfortable, even tormenting, to see this depiction of the world and to feel himself to be a part of the changes for which he had offered no approval.

He awoke from these scenes as if from a fearsome dream and ran from the edge of the mountain lest he see more than his mind could handle.

Elijah wondered what had happened to the

beauty he saw upon his initial arrival at the summit and, as he tentatively returned to the view from which he had just run, he saw that it was still there. But for how long? He felt brave in stepping back to the edge, this precipice of life and death, but his need for the reassurance it had previously provided became all-encompassing.

He looked across the skies once again and noticed that those rain clouds were approaching fast, blazing a trail across the sky just like the advance of the white man into indigenous lands. He wanted nothing more than for this to be madness, but felt in the deepest recesses of his mind that it was a clear-sighted message of what the future had in store for the people of the New World.

Saddened by his very self, the colour of his skin and all that it represented, he knew he needed to share this vision with those who had sent him here, but he was afraid to speak his truth as well. In this world nothing seemed less welcome than the truth.

The oppression of innocent cultures by the powerful started as a tool of class and might, but as foreign lands were conquered took the easy form of racism. Such low, divisive thinking disgusted Elijah: both equality and truth, closely tied as they are, had been left by the wayside somewhere along the journey of human development.

Would he be rejected, labelled mad or worse? How would he phrase such remarkable insights in a way that would not endanger his life, being a part of the problem as he was? Could a man be a part of the problem even though he wanted so badly to find a solution? He felt like a well-intentioned parasite as a result of such blistering insights.

Elijah felt ashamed for trespassing on this sacred land, confused about his purpose in being here and lost like never before. He wished for a while that he was back in England underneath the grey skies and surrounded by the limitations that come with a dense population.

Out here in the wilderness the skies were as endless as his worries, and he wept bitterly in the midst of this sensory assault, wondering what the future held for him as an individual if this was what he was a part of.

After what had seemed an eternity of negative sensations he returned to an emotional equilibrium in which he could just about function. He could see the ominous rainclouds progressing and desperately wanted to be somewhere safe and warm, away from the screaming terror of what was yet to come; he wanted shelter from what is and what was yet to be.

But there was no escape, especially not here. He got up, dusted himself down and wiped the tears from his face. He again thought of Christ in his suffering, images of His bleeding body coming to Elijah's troubled mind. Rather than forsaking Jesus alone, perhaps God had forsaken us all. Was he on a dying planet, bereft of hope, part of a species with no respect for itself or any other life form?

He turned for a final look across the vast expanse of this most holy place of wisdom just in time to see lightning strike in the farthest realms of his line of eye. Danger seemed to surround him now, though he stood in almost the exact spot upon which he had found contentment previously.

The images he had seen lay heavy on his heart.

One minute he'd felt precious to God, the next he felt abandoned. Try as he might to conceal this feeling, it flew from its cage within him. His eyes told a story of solemn regret; in all truth a great many tears had been shed.

Understanding had been his torture chamber; was it better to be emotionally numb and comprehensively blind? Sometimes Elijah wondered about the ignorance that accompanied the primary state of the human experience, but now didn't seem the appropriate time for such abstract dwellings.

Elijah decided he had seen enough, perhaps too much. He began to descend the mountain, his footing as unsure as his perceptions. Perhaps it was lack of nourishment or sleep that had driven him to his point, he thought. Perhaps it was something else.

Step by step he made his way downwards and with each passing moment the enormity of what he had just experienced truly dawned on him.

PART THREE:
After The Vision

A Moment Of Perfection

Chapter One

Back in the village, Elijah thought about how he would relay this apocalyptic nightmare to the Shaman. He felt an intuitive trust in the man, as though the Shaman saw through to his very soul and could perceive clearer than him the love which lay there.

The journey back had been arduous: many times he had taken a wrong turn and had to go back on himself and without an adequate supply of food he had felt ill in mind, body and spirit the whole way. It had taken him days to recover upon reaching the tribe; bruised and bloody was the condition he found himself in as he awoke from his coma-like state.

Now Elijah fumbled for the right words to express his truth before they were translated for the Shaman to understand. It started as a fog, a mist of interpretation. Then came a trickle of deep understanding. All of a sudden it burst from him: the truth in all its naked horror. The Shaman was shocked, saddened by these tales of quiet and loud desperation. He sat by Elijah's side and listened patiently for the vision to unfurl.

Elijah told it well: starting with the human world he weaved long trails of thought around certain themes such as racism, misguided ambition and avarice. The Shaman recognised these traits from his interaction with the invaders, who always thought their Gods were more powerful, their thoughts were more precious and their will unequivocally divine.

The Shaman had run away screaming from these interactions, but in Elijah he saw something different: a willingness to learn had overtaken the young Englishman's soul and he had come back from his adventure changed in all regards, visible and invisible.

Elijah was now more trusting of his tribal family, understanding as he did that they knew him already too well. He desperately wanted to put his mind back together after feeling it blown to pieces. Maybe the Shaman could provide the glue for his inner world's healing, Elijah pondered as he spoke.

"STOP!" The Shaman shouted in his tribal language, having heard more than enough.

"You mean the people of the future have no understanding that all things are one?" The

Spaniard translated these words for Elijah with touching sorrow.

"Almost none or only in theory."

"And they do not revere the great Mother Earth as provider of all sustenance?"

"Quite the opposite!"

It was as if Elijah were talking of completely foreign or unrecognisable concepts, a theory of life of which the Shaman had no comprehension.

Elijah continued.

"It looked as though the secret of life had been somehow lost through the ages,
peaking here and there in outrageous outbursts of creativity and ingenuity, but overall the ancient wisdom had seemingly deteriorated into something archaic and easily dismissed."

The Spaniard took his time to convey these ideas in the tribal tongue, wishing all the while they were easier to digest.

Elijah continued with his stark imagery, thinking that in sharing his concerns they would be perhaps halved.

"I could see cities of native peoples resigned to drink and poverty, downtrodden in the mud of history. I saw great warriors reduced to clowns in the circuses of the white man. I sensed the future of indigenous women, who disappeared in their thousands, hunted as prey by those ordained as supposed superiors.

I glimpsed the existences of the powerless and the powerful, who had grown completely foreign to one another; a vast chasm emerged between these two extremes. I saw minds confused about who was an enemy or friend, the line between the two becoming ever more blurry. I saw people divided by politics and religion, loath to believe the coin has more than one side."

The Shaman was shaken, distraught to hear of this world becoming so torn by divisions, so ripped apart by bad attitudes and to have drifted so far from its highest potential. This was not the depiction of what was yet to come that he had wanted or expected, and it was a struggle to assimilate these new insights into his already profound understanding of life. The elderly man resolved to fight against these features of the future wherever he could find them in what little time he had left and prayed that some wisdom would at least out-live him.

Chapter Two

Elijah was sent from the Shaman's hut to his place of rest. When he awoke the Shaman was gone and so too were most of the provisions. Elijah resolved to go hunting and set off with spear in hand. When he returned Adelita was waiting for him.

Three days later the lovers were disturbed by the Shaman's resurrection. Storming into the hut with no warning had its consequences and the Shaman could not un-see that which his eyes had revealed. In a fit he began to beat Adelita, showering her with guilt and reprimand until Elijah came between them.

"Don't touch her!" Elijah shouted. "She is with child."

At this the Shaman recoiled and reconciled his thoughts at this new information. He would have a new arrival in the tribe, half of native blood and half of the white man's. The Shaman conceded ground in the confrontation, emotionally transitioning with notable agility; he then retreated physically and left the lovers to their pleasure.

After the Shaman's initial rage had dissipated he had a breath-taking realisation: perhaps the vision he had seen long ago with the Englishman and a tribal woman had come to pass. Secretly he was happy for them. Love moves in mysterious ways - if you didn't know this, you didn't know much. He sincerely hoped there could be middle ground with this foreigner; perhaps, even after all, there could be harmony between their worlds.

He had come to think of Elijah as a son, distressed and distorted though he was. We are all imperfect, as the Shaman reminded himself every day. The Shaman decided to hold a smoke ceremony and ask the spirits what they had to tell him this day. He lit a fire and began to inhale deep plumes of various substances. Soon his vision began to change and, eyes closed, he began to see.

As images of vague shape and form started to clarify themselves, he saw an old man sitting by the riverside, surrounded by trees, light and peace. He wished he was seeing himself, but when the old man turned around the face was familiar though not his own.

It was Elijah who came to him in a dream, just

as he had many moons ago. Who was this special, peculiar person who now permeated his days? Could he achieve the peace, inner and outer, that so many desire? The Shaman concluded there was a star, perhaps a constellation of stars, watching over this young man, for he had come so far on so little hope.

Two dreams later and the Shaman was concerned to keep hold of the Englishman. He had the eyes of the Gods directly looking at him and the Shaman wanted a share of the spiritual spoils. He resolved to teach Elijah the ways of the tribe and in growing as he would, Elijah could become a treasured connection in their web of allies.

The tribal community was very remote, but invaders were becoming increasingly frequent. Elijah could prove useful with translation and interaction, understanding something of the white man's ways and destiny, if he was correct.

The Shaman felt an innate trust in this young stranger, though; a knowledge beyond words, an unspeakable affiliation. He decided to welcome Elijah into the tribe with a formal ceremony.

Chapter Three

Elijah prepared for the induction ceremony with great diligence. He now had a collection of charms and relics which he used to pray to the God who had shown him so much, taken him so far.

There were skulls and stones, pieces of wood and memorabilia from his previous life all gathered on his shrine, which was hidden from the sun's light yet illuminated by the fire. This was quite the collection, covering a huge span of time and experience. It reminded him of who he was in this new land.

Among his spread was Elijah's diary, which he often looked upon, wondering what this next phase of existence would bring. But he felt it to be only right that he had accepted the kind offer extended by the Shaman.

When he was summoned to go to the wise man Elijah had felt trepidation: would he be berated for his relationship with Adelita, torn apart from the person he felt closest to in the world once again?

He prayed not.

Life was cheap in this new world and he was thankful for every tomorrow, although he continued to have one eye on the afterworld. Meanwhile his journey continued, and when he was ready he left his hut.

The Shaman then explained to him warmly that although the messages from beyond were not to his liking, the person they had been given to had shown himself to be worthy of praise and approval. Indeed, as the older man explained to his pupil, there had been more than one dream vision of his presence and the gifts that it brings.

Elijah desperately wanted to find a home, a place in which to do good and grow. The tribe provided him with everything he needed and he was surprised that his presence was so welcomed.

He must be protected by God to have come this far, Elijah surmised, and knew that despite the colour of his skin and the strangeness of his ways, he was a part of something bigger than himself for perhaps the first - or last - time.

Clean and covered only in splendour, Elijah felt the strength of his form and the litheness of his physique. Adelita had done much to help him love himself and in the coming years he hoped to return the favour.

Yet despite the beauty he was experiencing for the first time and the warmth he felt surrounded by Elijah continued to be plagued by his visions from the top of the sacred mountain. What would become of these people once his countrymen had their way? Would the forest itself and all its inhabitants also be swallowed by the hungry monster of human greed?

Now that he had found the treasures he had been looking for he made his vows in earnest. He would protect the tribe, hunt and gather to provide and remain loyal to even the least insightful member.

They gathered around the open fire and told stories from their past in sporadic Spanish to accommodate Elijah. Every now and then he heard the unfamiliar, guttural sounds of the native language, perhaps some insult hissed in frustration or a private word to a fellow tribesman.

The Shaman got out his showreel of European artefacts and wondered again what the future held. The bathers in the fire's light fell silent once the future was raised. No one had the words to make everything calm and good again once the subject had been breached and there was a real sense of dread among the camp.

Would nights like this really be a thing of the past one day or would a few rebels try to keep the dream of really living alive? They ate what they had killed that day, a feast arriving before them thanks to a multitude of chefs, all jostling for prominence around the precious stew. They used all that the jungle had bestowed upon them: hides and wooden accessories here and there, a testimony to nature's provisions.

Aside from the future they had nothing to worry about. Elijah soaked in his moment, fiercely proud of who he had become and what the tribe in general saw in him. He was fast becoming seen as a visionary of sorts; a seer of the future, no matter how bleak a picture it might be. He revelled in his new-found role and hoped his friends and helpers in the spirit world could see him now.

Chapter Four

It was several months after his induction into the tribe that Elijah started to feel his sense of self changing. He became worried and agitated by the slightest of sounds. There had been increasing clashes with foreign soldiers in the jungle nearby and the tribe were troubled by the unsettling combination of events happening around them.

Adelita was six months into her pregnancy and Elijah wondered if he could be the father he wanted to this child. He had his mother's devotion to fall back on, but the fate of his brother had shown Elijah that one-winged planes seldom fly straight.

What kind of world was he bringing this child into, anyway? He or she had at least been conceived with love, the relationship between the parents growing, if anything, over time. This got Elijah thinking: would this child, born of affection, succumb to horror as well? Ben's words, like an ancient ghoul, came back to haunt him now, and Elijah could only wish such fears (or insights) away in order to continue on his set path.

However, he began to feel increasingly uneasy, an unmistakeable sense of foreboding overcoming his equilibrium. Elijah decided to talk to his old friend, the Shaman, about what he felt and was relieved to receive some empathy. Having to talk always through a third party made private conversation awkward, but they continued anyway. The bruising Spaniard, a man he had come to know as Mateo, was by now adept at interpreting and transmitting words of all varieties.

Mateo had been but a boy when he had been found by the tribe alone not far from the beach. His companions had been killed by a neighbouring tribe and Mateo faced the world alone. They had found him crying fiercely beneath a tree of the ancients where the tribe came to bury their dead. Watching this strange and lost child mourning in the place where they also came to grieve was touching to the tribe, who soon encircled him. The act of surrounding the child was initially threatening, but by the time interaction with the young Mateo had occurred there was a sense of humane sympathy for the foreign child.

Mateo had not resisted and the boy had grown into a man in the company of his initial foes. He learnt and taught in equal measure and in no time he became so embroiled in the tribal community that he began to see his previous countrymen a enemies, using his experiences to either kill or dismiss the danger of the coming invaders.

"They are all fools, every last one of them! We can kill them all with our bare hands."

"Perhaps it is you who is the fool, Mateo. Where you came from can't be all bad. Surely we can befriend these strange people?"

This was the discussion that took place on many nights, wondering who will befriend and who will betray, and how to tell the difference.

Elijah had learnt Mateo's story in due course, but initially their interaction was predictably stuttered. It's funny, Elijah later perceived, that sometimes your friends become enemies and sometimes your enemies become friends.

That night the Shaman's lengthy reply eventually came to Elijah through Mateo, who conveyed the words with naked passion:

"I, too, am worried, Elijah. The invaders are

coming closer every day and we can only hold them off for so long. These men are not like you; they know nothing of your grace. They are merely blood hounds on a mission to inflict suffering on all that surrounds them. They are like a disease in the land, a plague we must all experience for reasons beyond our understanding."

Elijah nodded and felt ashamed again, perceiving himself to be in some way a part of the problem.

"Maybe I should leave the tribe and go home. Your people are suffering enough."

"Elijah, your home is HERE, with us," the Shaman insisted.

"Thank you, that is appreciated. But what if the soldiers come and destroy our land, our home, our people?"

"We cannot understand the reason behind all things. That doesn't mean there isn't one."

With this, the conversation drew to a close and Elijah prayed to see the vision of the creator. He only saw the same images of pain and destruction again and again, recycling them in his mind though he tried hard to wish such horror away. He felt his faith slipping as he contemplated it all: what kind of being would design this, leaving so many people unable to cope?

If God had been so present in his own life, so remarkably kind at times despite the sadness, why couldn't everyone prosper from their relationship with Him? It seemed so unfair.

Even Elijah's time with the tribe started to sour in his mind. Having seen such power, passion and devotion as he had witnessed in these surroundings he did not want the soldiers to come and destroy it. He wanted to fight for it.

Several times he had been wounded protecting the village. He was now covered in a litany of scars, inner and outer injuries which would take more than time could provide to fully heal. Feeling encircled, he would need a miracle to escape the torture and suffering of waiting to kill or be killed. He asked God to show him a way to the peace he so urgently required before the birth of his child and the changing of seasons.

Chapter Five

The tribal people and Elijah tolerated each other's miscalculations of life; they did not try to correct any perceived difference unless absolutely necessary. This was in contrast to most relationships Elijah had experienced, in which sooner or later one had to be proven right and the other wrong, one feeble and the other triumphant.

The tribesmen knew there was a difference in beliefs and spoke of the Earth in ways that were so reverential that it was completely eye-opening to Elijah, who had tried to teach them something of Christ on occasion.

One of those occasions took place round the fire one night when everyone was dancing and drumming. It was the middle of summer, though Elijah had lost track of the specifics of time and space. The air was humid during the day, but crisp at night when the winds would roam in the relative silence.

A young man, Ista, asked Elijah in the broken Spanish he had learnt from Mateo about his relationship with God. This startled Elijah quietly, for faith was a powerful and often private aspect of one's life and to have the jar so roughly torn open made Elijah feel as though his insides would soon be all over the floor.

He felt naked; Elijah knew the easiest option would be to deny any faith and feign interest in theirs, but something within him, deep down inside his soul, had always clung to truth. Elijah believed truth had its own power and that in aligning with it you were innately a force for good in the world.

So, the tentative questioning came: "Tell me about your God, Elijah. Have you a soul, white man?"

These words were said with humorous affection, but they were met with scorn. Elijah spoke quickly and cared not who understood.

"Of course I have a soul! Every man, woman and child here does, along with the seas and rivers and their currents. It doesn't matter whether your skin is white as light or black as night, there is at least a hint of soul in most things.

My soul is in the hands of God, my Lord, my master. The captain of all ships and source of all good, the one who guides me when I am lost and comes to find me when I have strayed from the path of the wise."

Mateo interjected in order to convey these complex, adult ideas to those who could not understand. The young warriors were forming a small crowd now, curious as they were about this foreigner and his strange ways. Though they did not comprehend all he had said even with a translator they continued to probe in their youthful and overly curious way.

"Ask him, Mateo: Who is God?"

Elijah answered emphatically, afraid of letting any of his uncertainties show. "God is love."

"What happens when you die?"

"That is between me and my maker."

Whether Elijah's answers were vague or specific, the questions kept on coming.

"How do you know what is good and bad?"

"You can feel it in your heart."

"Why do bad things happen in the world?" Another young tribesman chirped up in broken Spanish, testing his linguistic capabilities. He was aware there was a psychological dance in motion and wanted to take part.

"Garden Of Eden. The Fall Of Man. Our own sinful nature. There are many theories."

These concepts were lost on the young men, who looked instead to each other for clarification. Finally the last of the queries arrived, as broad and abstract as it was possible for a question to be.

"What do you believe?"

Elijah was growing tired of the internal prodding, but humoured his company with an answer they may or may not have understood.

"I believe every heart has a portion of bad and a portion of good, but not all is distributed evenly. Who knows why this is? But we must work hard so that by the end of our days our hearts are a little stronger, a little more open, than when we started our journey. God willing I am here to do that with you. My heart is open to you all and my place with you is something I treasure."

With Mateo's invaluable help the trying conversation drew to a close and the evening's entertainment continued.

However, at the dawn of another night came another question; this time from Adelita. She wanted to know if Elijah was going to marry her.

Elijah was astonished by the provocation of her query. It seemed all the tribe wanted to know a man who barely knew himself anymore. In his bravery he asked her there and then. Before the birth of their first child, a baby he felt sure to be a boy, Adelita was made his wife and just for a moment - the first time since he had reached the blessed summit of that sacred trail up the mountain - all seemed right and good.

Chapter Six

One day while out hunting Elijah came across three Spaniards in the jungle. They seemed lost, loudly making their way through the natural world with no awareness of its dangers. Elijah wondered whether to kill them on sight, but he had never killed a man before and feared liking the taste.

He almost allowed them to pass, missing as they were the direct route to the camp. But they soon spotted him and a fight ensued. Elijah was armed with his knives and his poisons as they had been armed by their wits. They were even better fighters than they looked and Elijah had anticipated the worst: as soon as he realised he had been seen he feared the end was near, but when the Spaniards finally had him in a position of submission, he begged for his life in Spanish.

"LET ME LIVE! PLEASE! LET ME LIVE!" Elijah begged, his defeat plain to see. Presuming him to be a being akin to the animals they hunted, this shocked the Spaniards, and they recoiled. Looking Elijah's primal form up and down they grew contorted in disgust and confusion.

"What do you know of life, savage?"

"I know much and I can teach you. What do you want to know?"

The Spaniards thought a moment before answering with complete honesty.

"I'd like to know where my next meal is coming from."

"Then I will take you fishing," Elijah offered.

The Spaniards looked at one another, investigating the extent of their mercy. These were strange territories and to employ the skills of someone who could navigate them seemed a sensible option. They could always kill him after they had eaten. So they set about sourcing their meal tentatively, with no informalities. Elijah was conscious the whole time that his life was in danger, but he had nowhere to run and no way to hide.

"You could be useful!" said the leader of the three, Juan, over dinner. Elijah smiled awkwardly, feeling himself to be prey.

"Take us to your leader, we have trades to make with him."

"I cannot do that." Elijah rejected the thoughts of what had been suggested, let alone the actions. Although some Spaniards had occasionally interacted with the tribe, fighters of this pedigree, with these intentions, were not to be welcomed casually into the fold.

The Spaniards looked at each other with complex expressions, communicating in subtle ways Elijah could not fully understand.

"We will find your village sooner or later. You may as well give us a warm welcome. Unless you want a violent one," Juan spoke finally.

At this it was Elijah's turn to think. He intuitively did not trust these people, knowing the recesses of their poisoned minds far too well - for their thoughts had been akin to his own not too long ago. More and then more they want, knowing not to pause as they quenched the thirst of their greed.

Elijah reflected again on the visions from the mountain, haunted by images he could not understand. It had been, in hindsight, the peak of his understanding of all that is. Although he could not comprehend all of the communication of the Spaniards, they too could not decipher him. Elijah's eyes, mind, even his very soul had beheld things which few mortals could fathom.

As the images flooded his fragile consciousness, he saw that these Spanish men would fit in well in that future, lost as they were inside and out. Indeed, they were a part of its formation; it scared Elijah to contemplate the trap in which he now found himself.

Elijah knew they were right, though. If he himself had found his way to the village, others would too. With his life at stake he made a bargain. He would return to the village, but come back to meet the men tomorrow with food and trades.

At this the men allowed him to leave too readily for Elijah's personal comfort: they had no desire to honour their part in the bargain. Still, he was in no position to negotiate and left in a rushed, purposeful fashion.

The Spaniards laughed later about the young Englishman's naivety, but in exchange for life people will offer most things - even their senses.

It's funny, Juan thought to himself, how easily trust can be earned and then broken, an often violent procedure that can destroy a heart, a life or a culture. Still, he paid his intellectual wanderings no mind and set out on Elijah's trail.

All the way back Elijah felt he was being followed, but saw no hint of anyone else around. He looked here and there for signs of company, scouring the trees like a madman and slowly turning 360 degrees sporadically in order to drink in the entirety of surroundings. He found nothing, no sign of encroachment, no hint of friend or foe.

When he finally reached the familiar huts and dwellings, huddled together under a clear night's sky, he felt anxious. He told the Shaman of the Spaniards and the plan to meet tomorrow. The Shaman had a limited number of positive experiences with Spaniards and wanted to make a good impression: he said he would prepare some gifts to offer the men who had spared his friend's life.

After his meeting with the tribal elder, Elijah went to find Adelita. As soon as he saw her all his pride dissipated and he instantly emotionally broke down. Having come so close to death, he could not imagine a journey to the afterworld without her and his child. He did not want to be as alone as he had been previously once again. His wife and unborn baby were a part of him now and they needed him to protect and provide for them as they continued to learn and grow.

The tribe lay down to sleep in the night when Elijah awoke to the sound of a piercing, terrified scream. He ventured out into the blackness and, though he could barely make out shape and form, he found the Spaniards attacking the village in seemingly large numbers. He knew who they were instantly with their armour and shouts. The men of the village were rallied and soon there was a fight for survival taking place unlike any the tribe had seen.

Many women were attacked and men were dying to defend them all around. The children screamed and danced between swords. Eventually the whole tribe worked together to drive the wave of foreigners back into the darkness, though victory came at a heavy price. Despite the Shaman remaining mysteriously unharmed, many of Elijah's friends – including some of the young warriors who had accosted him at the fireplace on many nights - had been summoned by the spirit world, their journeys transferred to another realm.

The Spaniards crawled back into the darkness, stung by their defeat. Yet they would not give up: with greater numbers and resolve, they planned to return to the camp as soon as they had gathered their strength.

An emergency meeting was called, with every able-bodied member of the tribe present. The remaining elderly and the wounded stayed away, but would hear of the decisions made by the tribe in the months to come: they decided to move deeper into the jungle, far from the grasping hands of affliction. That very day the preparations began, so that when the Spaniards returned in the subsequent nights the tribe had already moved on.

Elijah's prayers got all the more desperate. He knew not of his bearings. All seemed up that should be down, and left what used to be right. Having killed several men in a primal flurry fuelled by fear, he now had to accommodate his deeds in his own self-reflection.

No longer could he claim to be the Christian his God had intended him to be. Surrounded by alien deities and feeling a sense of disconnection deep within, he prayed the feverish prayers of a killer. He begged God for forgiveness, for grace. In this world of kill or be killed, he knew not the best option, though he yearned to understand the path of righteousness still. All he really comprehended was that others depended upon his survival for theirs, and thus a chain was created: a need for one another, a trust, a dependency. He must play his part, however bloody his hands were to become.

After a few days in a state of transition the tribe found a clearing and established themselves again over time. The whole area was new to most of them, not a home at all - yet. Their innate senses of teamwork and generosity were outstanding, Elijah noted, while accompanying the men of the tribe on mission after mission to find suitable materials for shelter as the women toiled and cooked.

The tribe had been heavily reduced by the attack, but forty remained, determined to see more summers and winters, the beauty of life all the more clear to them when juxtaposed by the indignity and cruelty of death.

Chapter Seven

Elijah still had problems with his mind, especially at night. He was terrified of another attack and aware of death's seemingly steady stare. One night it overwhelmed him and he spoke to Adelita about his inner world as though he could make her understand. "I'm just waking up from a dream ten times, unsure of what is real," he said to himself in English and then repeated to her in Spanish. She seemed to vaguely comprehend his plight.

Presuming Elijah to be struggling with the shadows of his past Adelita replied: "Your vision at the summit of the mountain was an experience, but you don't have to let it define you." Elijah appreciated the comforting tone, but he doubted whether Adelita could fully fathom the landscape of his emotional nadir.

Elijah knew the Shaman understood and they shared a deep inner knowing between them with regards to each other's thoughts, deeds and emotions. Elijah would wonder to himself whether he had found the father figure he had always wanted, but the respect he had for his friend went far beyond that he had felt towards his own father.

It was an entirely new experience for Elijah: he had found someone to learn from, look up to and follow. Should the wise man ever ask anything from him other than to co-exist Elijah would move the heavens to make it so. As the fears of the two men grew, so too did their relationship, and each moved towards the other as a flower reaches for the light. Both had a truth which was hard to put into words, both wanted to see how the other saw, each lay awake on the same shared nights asking simultaneously which way to turn.

It had been hard leaving their home and making a new environment their own, but each member of the tribe played a part in their collective survival. Especially with depleted numbers, people worked themselves to illness trying to help the tribe to function. Food could be scarce and there was a terror involved in venturing too far from the hub of things, lest they should find more trouble.

Surrounded, cowering and afraid, the tribe lived on. Maya Keith, as Elijah had named her to the confusion of the tribe, was born in the height of summer, just as the Sun claimed its throne. Indeed, the tribe were so confused by the last name that Maya became known as "Mayakeith" by many members of the tribal community. Elijah approved and, although he had been expecting a son, the girl child emerged as a thoughtful, but demanding, addition to the tribe.

Chapter Eight

"Truth, virtue, justice:
It's a suicide machine.
I cut myself on pieces of reality."

These were the last words Elijah scrawled in the few worn remaining pages of his diary before the attack came. Unbeknownst to him they would be the last sentences he would ever write, his words soon lost to the corrosive sea of time.

It had been in the middle of the day when the hunters warned of the presence of enemy forces nearby. Within hours there was an ambush and the tribe, so deep in the jungle foliage and trying to live without the warriors of previous times, was quickly and easily overwhelmed. In no time Elijah and the other men of the village had been surrounded and there was no escaping the excess of numbers thickly layered against them.

"Why are you doing this? Can you not leave us in peace? What do you want from us?" Elijah called in Spanish, as the forces of darkness gathered around them.

"This is now our land. Do not resist. You will work in the mines near here and bring us what you find. If you don't agree to this kind offer we will have no alternative but to kill you all."

Elijah was incensed. "So we work for you or die? That seems like a living death to me!"

At this Elijah was silenced by the Shaman who raised his stick as a gesture he was about to speak.

"You have come into our home, you have scared our children, you have threatened our women. For what? What is your purpose?" The Shaman spoke in his native tongue and the Spaniards looked at one another inquisitively until a translation emerged. Though clearly in the right, the tribal elder seemed visibly shaken.

The leader of the marauding Spaniards then introduced himself.

"I am Captain Carlos. As my colleague explained, this is our land now. You may work for us or perish. The choice is yours."

The tribal members looked at each other and, despite Elijah's big words, agreed to do some work for the invaders.

Elijah spat at the feet of the Captain.

"I will never work for you, vermin!"

With that he was taken and restrained by the unrelenting sea of foreign faces. Elijah found himself tied to a tree and thought his throat would be cut. Yet he knew his time had been up several times over at that point, and did not fear another brush with the afterlife.

The Shaman looked on aghast and helpless against the impact of his friend's suffering. The tribe was taken into slavery and made refugees in their own land. Knowing how to hunt and survive had ultimately proved unimpressive to these invaders, who simply wanted to take what they could and found some people in the way.

The first day of mining was devastating for the tribe. Even the women and children were put to work, Adelita cuddling her infant to her chest as she beat against the elements according to the instructions of strangers. Too weak to stand by the end of the day, she collapsed in a pool of tears and despair. Elijah could not comfort her, tied as he was to the tree for two days. Drunk with exhaustion, he was finally cut down and persuaded to mine with the others.

Every day he planned his escape, every minute he thought of Adelita and his daughter and how to free them. Then one day he got his chance: the enemy soldiers had left their swords and guns to one side in order to bathe in the river. Elijah immediately saw his opportunity, killed whoever he could and then begged God for forgiveness.

Alone and armed, Elijah wondered with wild eyes how to help the others. He ran as far as he could and aimed to return in the coming days in order to help his family and friends regain their freedom. In the middle of the night he heard men scouring the jungle, presumably looking for the escapee. Elijah camouflaged himself with leaves and hid up a tree, hoping they couldn't sense him from below as he watched the enemy pass. Soldier after soldier, like insects, they passed. All bloodthirsty, all craving their next kill, all asleep to the impact of their cruelty.

Elijah couldn't leave his family and he devised various plans to visit the mines, but each time

237

he got closer to its location more soldiers appeared. He had tumbled into a bitter world, where good men were hard to find; he felt lost, alone and desperate in every sense. In the darkness he fished, though it was difficult to see and every sound made his fear of being found increase. But when at last he caught something he made a fire and cooked the flesh, far enough away from everything to really think.

He was alone once more - except for the stars - and praying for redemption. It was one of the times in life when tomorrow seemed unclear, let alone anything further ahead. Had the future he envisaged at the summit of the mountain come early? Could he ever make his way back to a time when all seemed right and good?

As he devoured the fish he thought of his great rage at the people who had destroyed his new home, taken the tribal lands and ripped him from his family. The resentment burned inside him, his anger like a hot stone he was holding on to for dear life, afraid of what he'd feel were it not for his wrath. It was enough to make him as murderous and deadly as the other invaders, enough to make Elijah feel he could kill ten men before sunrise and run into the sunset with his family intact.

238

But where would they go? There was nothing left for them here and deep in his heart Elijah knew that it was all over, a dream too sweet and blessed to be real.

Chapter Nine

Adelita struggled in the mine as a mother and a slave, but mostly as a woman. The Spanish officers surrounded her with hungry eyes and if she wasn't perspiring from working then she sweated with sheer fear of what was to come. She had heard of Elijah's escape and wondered whether he would come back for her, but the sense of imprisonment only increased with each passing day.

"You! What are you thinking? Focus on your work!" a Spaniard bellowed, unashamed of his brutality.

The words were accompanied by several lashes on her back and shoulders, narrowly missing Maya as Adelita shielded her. The child started to cry, feeling her mother's pain as though the umbilical cord connected them still. Adelita had no one to protect her now. Her pain at her situation ate her up inside, gnawing and wearing away any resolve she had to continue. But when she looked into Maya's eyes and saw herself and her love combined she knew she had to go on. Pushing past every limit of endurance she had ever felt, she chipped and measured as she had been instructed to do.

In between her work Adelita took short, monitored breaks to breastfeed her young child, though the milk her offspring relied upon had become a trickle as opposed to the stream it was intended to be. With no one seemingly by her side to help her and the connections of the tribal community worn and frayed, her life was not what the young woman had hoped for. Finally she passed out while working and was taken for treatment, Maya screaming in her mother's lifeless arms.

Chapter Ten

Waking early in the morning and bathing in the river, Elijah thought he heard Adelita's cry. At the very same moment her pained voice echoed through his soul the birds took flight and scared him. It was time to act, to fulfil the duty his love for her had bound him to. Quickly gathering his things, he prepared for a short but perilous journey. He skilfully plotted and schemed his way closer to the mine, still armed with the weapons he had stolen and the wits he had honed over the course of his time as a hunter and gatherer.

He approached the encampment with exquisite caution - it had taken him days to get so close. What he saw through the clearing, under the cover of the last trees, was heart-breaking. The same faces he had known as free men were now drawn and haggard, weighed down by the impossibility of their situation.

The humble mountain that the mine surrounded was a sad shadow of its previous self. Worn and corroded by the excavations, it stood like a man with half a leg missing. The Spaniards clearly had no respect for the land or its people.

Mixed with the familiar faces were the unknowns: those from other neighbouring tribes, previously considered enemies themselves, who had also been brought into the fold of the foreigners. Elijah felt nothing but contempt when he looked upon the scene. The mine was a cavernous opening in an until-then pristine mountain, but since resources had been found there which the white people wanted – silver, especially - it had become a location for pain and suffering.

He knew the odds of rescuing anyone else in order to take them away from this place and reproduce what they once had were non-existent. It was all Elijah could do to keep himself from weeping, but he knew he had no time to cry as the soldiers circled closer to his lair.

Chapter Eleven

Lost, alone and in many ways broken, Elijah
chose to wreak vengeance upon the invaders.
Killing indiscriminately and almost for pleasure,
his reputation grew before him. Some talked of
a madman of the jungle. Others, presuming the
enemy to be more numerous, spoke of a tribe
that was yet to be tamed. Either way, the
dangers of the New World remained imminent
and terrifying.

Elijah, too, was petrified. Yes, he could kill and
kill he did, but he could not save the family and
friends he had made from their fates.

Sometimes he wished they had all perished and
then none of this would have been possible.
They would have all been resting with the
angels, belief or no belief. At least that's what
Elijah thought on lonesome nights, surrounded
by conflict, disorder and sorrow.

It was a time when life seemed barely
preferable to death. Many times he thought of
taking his own life, so ashamed was he of his
situation, so hopeless his predicament seemed
to be to him. But while there was strength in his

limbs and eyes to see the damage these people were doing he resolved himself to fight it.

Every now and then he would sneak back to the mine, when he could, to take a look at what was happening there. The sights which met him conjured images from the top of the sacred mountain, and he could not look for long. He never saw his family or friends, maybe would never again. So numerous were the tribesmen that one face blurred into another, faces of desperation and bleak resignation.

The killing continued on both sides. The invaders were keen on more territory, more resources and cared not who stood in their way. Elijah was aware of the need for justice, redemption and reprieve. He didn't think too much about those he killed. Their journeys to the afterlife were as foreign to him as many of their languages. As time went on he heard Dutch, Portuguese, Spanish, French… a chorus of foreign tongues. Though truth had been a burden almost too heavy to carry, he continued to pray for his redemption and guidance from the God that had shown him so much.

In his bitter moments Elijah resented his faith, guiding him as it had to moments which he did not want to be a part of. Troubled times, filled with insights which had been given to him so quickly, with such force, that he felt his cup of understanding might overflow.

Those Elijah killed were not so fortunate, it was clear. All too often their lack of knowledge of their environment and its perils left them stranded and foolish, easy to divide and hunt like the prey Elijah would feed on.

As well as learning how to kill, Elijah even knew when. Sometimes he would let the invaders pass, their numbers too many and their rifles too searching. It was all he could do not to be seen. Yet when the numbers were low and the rifles less probing Elijah knew the soft parts of the flesh, the fragility of the human form.

At times he felt remorse for his new-found life as a blood-soaked protector of the realm, but also that he had no choice: he had reached the conclusion that evil was better dead than alive. He struggled with moral dilemmas from his youth which would haunt him along with his now extensive collection of ghosts. He knew how disgusted God was by murder, and yet he had seemingly been put in a world where there was little choice in the matter. Elijah's enemies had stolen everything from him, his new-found people and their land. When and where would they stop?

Elijah concluded that the dance between good and evil, black and white, men and women, right and wrong would never end, just mutate throughout time and space. Still, he wanted to ensure that he was on the right side, and continued to pray for redemption from his sinning ways whenever he found a suitably tranquil moment.

Yet even a fleeting glimpse of calm solitude was now hard to find. He hungered for the sense of peace he had found at the summit of the sacred mountain, surrounded as he now was by danger and strife. His skills could take him so far, but they couldn't save those he loved. He was tormented by his own feebleness and limitations as a human being.

Yet his skillset was growing with every day that passed. He had become highly adept in his pursuit of his enemies, knowing when to come and when to flee, when to attack from a height or when to face them in hand-to-hand combat. Many had caught sight of this madman of the jungle and spoken of his fearsome appearance to colleagues. Word spread among the soldiers that the area surrounding the mine was a fearful one, yet increasing numbers of men would meet their end trying to navigate the inhospitable terrain.

The enemy were annoyed by these instances, but little more. They were too busy soaking in the glory of their finds in the mine. Silver was plentiful, along with other rare jewels and resources, and the haul was packed up to be sent back to Europe.

Unfortunately for the invaders, there was a cross-over at some point: the men who carried the treasure to the ships were intercepted with increasing frequency, leaving Elijah to find the fruits of the labour of his loved ones. Sickened by the sight, he began to hoard the findings and discovered in doing so a streak of his character that was alike to those he killed.

Time soon revealed to him that he liked the shine of the silver, the accumulation of riches, the feelings which came with these new possessions. But he knew not what to do with them all, so he kept them in a safe place near the river, buried under enough earth to be hidden from those who travelled over it.

Chapter Twelve

Adelita's hair may well have been matted, her eyes as wild as an animal in a snare. But she still fought the tears of each day. With everything she had, she fought them. Through the wind, rain and sun she continued on, the love in her chest her only guide.

Like most subtly great people, she was wracked by insecurities. Constantly waiting to see if the next meal arrived, she was amazed her eyes opened in the morning. Though she did her best for herself and Maya, she knew not where to put her feet from one step to the next.

Day after day she would wonder about Elijah. Where was he? Was he dead? Had he forgotten her and his daughter, along with all of the memories they shared? Ever since she had heard that he had escaped the mine these questions had troubled her. She thought they would punish her should they know their connection, but nothing happened.

Indeed, there was a wilful ignorance of all tribal ways, relationships and culture. Adelita observed that the Spaniards possessed a

249

visceral distain for all things native, a sneering distinction between the European's ways and those of the darker people they encountered. Yet all around there was now no hint of anything except the destruction of human beings, nature and the respect for the divine.

Where was Elijah to talk to of such things, this great visionary who had seen nightmares beyond description? Adelita did not know whether to mourn him, what to think of his actions (though she knew of them not). She felt her blindness would drive her crazy. Day after day trying to raise her child amidst this chaos, it was no easy life.

Adelita looked for the Shaman sometimes for signs of leadership or escape, but all she found was a spindly frame and a hollowness of the face. All the tribe now wore the same mask of misery, the same clothes as rags. Gone were the days of full bellies and open fires, and it pained Adelita to think of the past. She also knew she had to remember that in this world of pain and grief, she had for a fleeting second found something sacred.

Elijah had too. He had spoken of it: the harmony of all things, if respected. Perhaps this was why they had understood each other so well. Now the new life her love had birthed looked up at her as if she had the answers, as if the magic still resided in her. Adelita felt as though all her spells had been cast, however; she now knew the answer to very few questions.

Chapter Thirteen

Captain Carlos sat back and greedily poured himself another generous portion of alcohol. The natives were growing more numerous by the day. Who knew how long the officers could keep order? The stress was starting to get to him. All those primal people with their hungry eyes and demonic ways. They knew nothing of Jesus although he had tried to convert a couple of them. The Captain had so badly wanted to teach them the ways of civilisation. The tribesmen just looked at him with sunken faces, skin dark as the night and eyes searching for the truth.

"You wouldn't know the truth if it bit you," he spoke out loud, though there was no one in the room.

The truth, the Captain pondered, was a washerwoman working too late at night, wondering what tomorrow will bring. She sweated and toiled, but try as she might she'd never get her garments clean.

The children were a concern, too. He didn't want to kill them all in case their parents stopped working, but they sure did get in the way. If only there was some way to school them, teach them the arts and how to behave with respect for their superiors. They would learn of Christ and his kindness if it kills them, he thought! But for now there was only profit to think of and the mines were making plenty. More slaves were arriving every day, forced into a life of servitude and tacit greed.

He wondered where it would end, arranging his mind into a myriad of different options and formations; he twisted reality with childish enthusiasm, knowing not what would finally fall into place and become lived experience. Right on the precipice of existence was where he laid his head, yearning and searching for direction. As long as the mine's outgoings were sufficient nothing else mattered. He knew his place with or without visions of what might be.

He took his boots off his aching feet and thought what a miserable life he had. Swigging thirstily from his bottle now and bemoaning his aches and pains, he washed the residue of blood from his hands. The Captain had no option but to kill a slave for not minding his tongue when he spoke to his superior officer. The native was from one of the unruly tribes, always a pain. Once the tribesman started to threaten him a line had to be drawn: these people had no respect.

"Your time will come," the tribesman had said to Captain Carlos, one of the translators from the tribe who now worked with the Spanish interpreted it. Oh, the insolence! Oh, the shame! The savage words now rang in his ears.

Chapter Fourteen

It was the middle of the afternoon, during the height of the sun's illuminating power when Elijah heard the unmistakable sounds of a trail through the foliage. Sneaking up unannounced he saw there were three, maybe four, Englishmen in shining uniforms attempting safe passage to an unknown destination. Perhaps it was unknown to the soldiers themselves. Perhaps it was the mine.

Elijah had grown cocky in his merciless attempts at the administration of a warped kind of justice. He felt confident that he would be the victor at any time of day or night. Pistols and poisoned arrows featured among Elijah's now vast array of weaponry.

Indeed, soon three of the companions were dead. The other proved harder to find. Eyes wild and blood boiling, Elijah scanned the natural world for signs of human presence. The soldier finally tried his luck: he shot at Elijah, but missed badly and only alerted his enemy to his location. Elijah easily put an end to the challenge with a poisoned arrow directed right at his countryman's torso. Within seconds it had pierced right through his flimsy shirt and taken effect while Elijah hid and anticipated his conquest; the challenge was once again no more.

Elijah couldn't help but approach the soldier, morbidly looking for signs of life. Creeping forward tentatively, he arrived to find only the soulless shell of a corpse. Ignoring the copious signs of a vacated being, the terrified eyes and the twisted limbs, the soldier was a fine young specimen of a man. Elijah gorged on the sight, but soon found he could look no longer: he was only seeing a ghost of his former self.

It was during these moments, feeling ambivalent about his actions and their deadly consequences, that Elijah had a sense of clear vision. He realised he could steal this Englishman's uniform and dress as though he was a part of the expected expedition. Were he to cut his hair and shave his beard he would be unrecognisable to those who manned the mines, and it had been long enough now that the personnel would have presumably changed many times.

After stealing yet more of the Englishmen's resources Elijah devised a plan to enter the mining settlement, buy as many 'slaves' as possible and escape where they would, living again as free people. At this Elijah became elated, dancing maniacally before simpering in wonder. He then shaved and cut his hair before trying on his outfit, a tricky business of stolen razors and trying to remember old skills. He looked at his reflection in the stillness of the river and again saw a phantom of his former self. It scared him. His young face looked more worn than last time he'd seen it, cut here and there by bad shaving. Still, it would have to do.

The treasures, however, were more difficult to arrange. There were a lot. He would have to make several trips to the camp in order to carry it all, but he didn't trust anyone to accompany him either side of the journey. He didn't want to lead them to his secret hoarding place and he didn't want to leave treasure unattended while he went back for more. The only way forward was to take as much as he could carry and see if he could strike a bargain with the mine's chain of command.

Elijah dressed himself the very next morning as if going into battle. His uniform seemed to gleam as his skin stung in the morning sun. He gathered as many of his riches as he could carry and made a plan in his mind, sometimes speaking his ideas out loud in his rusty English until he was sure he had a chance.

All he needed was an opportunity to redeem himself before the eyes of his God: it was Elijah who led the Spaniards to the village, it was Elijah who had brought these people an image of the future without hope or redemption. Perhaps their own minds were fuelling the creation of a netherworld before their eyes, worrying and fretting until their fears became real.

No matter what the cause, the effect was plain to see. Elijah hated the thought of the love of his life behind barriers and restricted when, like Mother Nature or Venus or Eve incarnate, Adelita was born to be free. He hated the thought of the Shaman and his wisdom falling on deaf ears. He hated to think of the young warriors using their waning strength and vitality for the wrong cause. He most of all couldn't bear his own reflection knowing they were suffering while he was free. There was no alternative: for this he would give his life, lay down his soul, surrender to something more than himself.

Elijah took to praying before the journey, bending his knees in pious reflection. He wanted more than ever to help those who had taught him so much and asked God to guide his footsteps, words and deeds. He would need all the help, luck and protection in the known world – which he was at the edge of now – for this to succeed. It was a new brand of audacity exhibited by Elijah. In short, these were the actions of a man on the brink of not wanting to live.

Objectively, you could say Elijah had lost his mind, but the truth was he was far beyond that. He had transcended: he now wandered in a realm far beyond good and evil, sane and insane, right and wrong. One could say death was always at his side, that he was all too familiar with the sensations of loss. Though he awoke in the morning (and sometimes the depth of the night), he often would wonder: How? Why? What had awakened him into this world of danger and fear? Elijah felt resentment towards the God that had led him to this point: in short, he felt totally abandoned.

Risking his life on another foolish mission just seemed the right thing to do. After all, even if he had to exchange his life for some spiritual redemption at this point he would have done a good thing: the bargain would be his.

Chapter Fifteen

From deep in the heart of the jungle Elijah travelled to the mine, nervous about making a good impression to these devils. As he approached guns gathered in the trees, arched expertly towards Elijah's fast-beating heart. The leaves crunched under his feet, the twigs broke according to his footsteps. Every noise made him nervous, but he knew he was not alone.

"I have come to trade," Elijah shouted in Spanish, trying to ensure his voice did not shake. Behind their natural visual protection the Spaniards looked at one another. The obvious foreign accent betrayed Elijah's vulnerability; the Spaniards would have shot there and then were it not for their incessant greed.

"I have more where this came from!" Elijah said opening the chest he had brought with him. Through the trees the Spaniards' eyes widened. They were suspicious of this young buck in his English uniform.

"WAIT! DO NOT GO ANY FUTHER!" Elijah heard a strong Spanish voice bellow.

It was at this point that one of the soldiers ventured out from his cover to confront Elijah.

"What are you talking about, madman? Do you know where you are?"

Elijah went with his planned proposition: "I am the only survivor of my crew after an attack by natives. I have buried all of our immense treasure and would like to" – Elijah almost said "sell it back to you", but just about stopped himself by coughing – "exchange these riches for some slaves. I hear they are plentiful here?"

Elijah awaited their response with beads of sweat gathering on his forehead and upper lip, trickling down into his eyes and mouth.

Chapter Sixteen

Jose, an adolescent Spaniard, burst into Captain Carlos' office to find the commander pouring himself yet another drink.

"BOY! Haven't I warned you about this before? Do you want a lashing to remind you of my instructions? DON'T COME IN BEFORE YOU KNOCK: I MAY BE BUSY!"

"Clearly," thought Jose, though he was too afraid to speak his mind.

"Sir, we have an issue. An Englishman is asking to trade, says he brings many riches, says he wants some slaves…" The young man stumbled over his words just like a child, which annoyed the Captain even further.

"Rich people always want more slaves, son." Captain Carlos mumbled his speech as he took a swig of his stiff drink.

"Kill him and steal his treasure. What's his life to me?"

"He says he has more, but has yet to bring it."

"He's a liar, a madman or worse!"

"Yes, sir," Jose agreed too readily for the Captain's liking, as though he hadn't given himself time to hear what was said before voicing his support.

Captain Carlos considered him for a moment, a charmless slip of a boy; not enough meat to even justify eating him. Out of curiosity or just to rid himself of Jose's increasingly unbearable presence, he finally slurred his answer.

"Bring him to me."

Jose nearly tripped over himself on his way out, momentarily cartwheeling and swaying wildly. But after regaining his balance he managed to exit the anxious scene with his life, if not his pride, intact.

Chapter Seventeen

As Elijah waited still amidst the looming trees for an answer from the Spaniards, he felt his soul slip out through his feet and view the scene from above. What a fool he was, believing he could see his loved ones again, having faith in the power of his own beliefs, thinking anything good could happen. Then the answer came. He was waved forwards by the Spanish troops who slowly started to show themselves as he drew ever nearer. There were more of them than Elijah thought, perhaps twenty; he would never be able to fight his way out of this situation alone, even with all his righteous rage.

He was led towards the mine and, as the gates opened, Elijah felt a dreadful sense of foreboding: this was the line past which no good man was free, this was the point at which all dreams end, this was where previously free people come to die, Elijah surmised. He wondered whether he would be with the angels too before the day's end.

Elijah was ushered to a small shack and was alarmed to find himself face-to-face with none other than Captain Carlos, the man who had, a seeming eternity ago, tied him to a tree for days forcing him to dwell silently upon his own mortality. It took Elijah no time to recognise him as he tried to supress his anxieties, but to his relief the feeling was not reciprocated. As the Captain stood for him uneasily, even gently swaying, Elijah introduced himself.

"Good afternoon, sir. My name is John Cane. I was part of an expedition which has now come to an end, but I have managed to retain many treasures and I would like to buy some slaves in order to rebuild my position," Elijah spoke with all the steadiness and authority he could muster.

The Captain looked him up and down suspiciously. Elijah proceeded to open his treasure chest with slightly shaky hands in order to sway the situation. He damned his nerves for betraying him – where was his composure when he needed it most? It was all Elijah could do not to drop the loot all over the Spaniard's dusty floor. With the glistening jewels in his eyes the drunken officer was persuaded.

Slurring his reply, the officer seemed numb to any hint of deception. "You may have four natives for your troubles, boy. You say you have more where this came from?"

"I have more. I will take five for this price."

The Captain growled and finally hissed his reply: "As you wish!"

The natives had been nothing but trouble for Captain Carlos since he had encountered them. He had seen the scowling looks and heard the rumours of uprisings. What were a few less savage to worry about?

As Elijah moved forwards and placed his treasure on the table, relieved to not have to showcase it any more with his trembling grip, the Captain noticed blood stains on the Englishman's uniform.

"From my struggles with the natives," Elijah attempted to dismiss the official's concern, berating himself for not choosing a cleaner uniform. Flashes of the death of the man whose tailoring he wore flooded his mind; he suddenly felt like the liar and murderer he had now so obviously become. He worked hard not to let his inner shame show and continued with the communicative pitter-patter that the Captain felt comfortable with.

After another drink for the Spanish officer, they went together to pick out five fortunate souls to leave this camp and never return. Destitute faces peered up at Elijah and pleaded for their lives to change. Elijah walked past them. When he spotted Ista he stopped. "This man," Elijah said to the Captain. "Very well," the Captain said and moved the young tribesman to the side.

Ista did not know what was happening, but felt intuitively that being singled out could not be good. He started to protest. Elijah leaned in to the situation and said. "Quiet, boy. You're coming with me." Ista realised as soon as he looked into Elijah's eyes that his friend had returned. He was speechless in the face of this realisation. A wink let Ista know it was the hour of his redemption.

Next Elijah saw the stooped and weary figures of various strangers, and tried to feign interest while awaiting another familiar face. The features of these people had changed so much in the short time he had been away: their eyes were now hollow or full of fear. He had trouble recognising anyone, and tried not to let his increasing desperation show.

Then Elijah saw her, panting heavily on the edge of the crowd. Adelita had recognised Elijah straight away, would know his walk and talk anywhere. Her eyes were heavy with un-shed tears, yearning as she'd been for this moment. She was so overwhelmed by emotion that she nearly cried his name. However, looking at the situation she knew instantly that her place was to let him find her, the one he had been hoping to reach.

Their eyes met and tears welled within them, though their verbal communication betrayed nothing of the sort. Adelita maintained her restrained silence, glancing all around her as if drinking in this fateful scene, while Elijah muttered to the Captain about his need for a woman.

"This one. I want this one," Elijah spoke with conviction.

"She comes with child."

"I will pay for both."

The Spaniards looked at one another quizzically, having been certain that the child would be a deal-breaker. The tribal people were

269

no loss to the keepers of the mine, however; one less hungry mouth to feed, as they often would say when a native died or escaped. They had even said this about Elijah. But now Elijah was reaping the rewards of an ambitious, far-reaching mind combined with a spiritual purpose: he was granted Adelita and Maya in a moment that lifted him high above his concerns for the future.

Elijah saw another familiar figure looming large in the crowd of pleading faces. Matzika stood taller than all the rest, so Elijah couldn't understand how he had not seen him sooner. Perhaps his emotions were starting to get the better of him, too.

"That man in the middle," Elijah said and pointed. Matzika's muscles had all but deflated and gone was the cheek of his previous self. Elijah would have known his friend anywhere, though, and felt elated to be in his presence once again. Matzika was directed towards the spot where Ista, Adelita and Maya had gathered.

"One more," declared Captain Carlos.

"This one," Elijah said, mimicking the callousness of his enemies, trying to seem at one with them whilst only wanting to run and embrace his wife and child. He had been waiting for this moment. Elijah had pointed straight at the Shaman.

"Not this one. He has the eye of spirit. The men are afraid of him," Captain Carlos returned. Elijah pleaded, but to no avail. He looked at his dearest friend, who returned his stare and gently shook his head.

"I will give the young boy back, should you let me take this one."

Ista looked nervous amidst the collection of natives cast aside. Having been promised freedom he would not settle for less. Having promised the young tribesman his place in the scheme, Elijah was saved from the shame of reneging on this agreement by Captain Carlos' reply.

"I told you: this one's not for sale," the Captain confirmed.

Ista breathed a sigh of relief. But a tension was evident between the two central men regarding their bargaining. Elijah wanted to slit the Captain's throat, but instead he remembered his manners. "As you wish," he said through gritted teeth, though he was silently devastated not to be able to rescue his great companion.

Elijah saw several more familiar faces amidst the crowd, who had now started to gossip among themselves so loudly that the Captain called for quiet. Finally he chose Mana, the spiritual woman with great healing powers which Elijah had borne witness to on occasion. He thought Adelita might need some female company to help them raise Maya. In truth, he didn't know what he was thinking. He was just exhilarated to have reached this point.

The deal was complete and the six were ushered towards the exit as though their continued presence was a burden. Elijah promised to return with further treasure one day soon, contagious lies continually falling from his mouth.

As they left the compound there were nervous thoughts among all five of the tribal members. When would they be able to stop the act and embrace as they knew they should? It took them several elongated minutes before Elijah turned to them with a smile that could light up a night: they were free again and rejoiced as only the free can.

The kiss Elijah gave Adelita, full of love and relief, expressed all of the emotion his words could not. Her love for life returned with his touch, though Maya continued to cry. The child could not partake in the beauty of the moment correctly, but without her cries there was not an inkling of pain to be found between all six of them. They were together again and for a fleeting moment all seemed right once more.

Chapter Eighteen

Matzika spoke of his beloved tribal companion's death for most of the passage towards the river. He explained that although Mazula's mind had been sound to the last, his body wasn't capable of withstanding the harsh treatment and gruelling hours of manual labour. He had succumbed to exhaustion shortly after Elijah had escaped. Now it was clear Matzika had taken it upon himself to share the memories of his friend lest they fall into the quicksand of time.

He spoke of hunting expeditions, deep conversations and Mazula's wisdom in terms of foraging and gathering. As Matzika continued on his monologue it began to rain. It was not a small shower: this kind of downpour could sweep away a man – or a young child.

Elijah held his baby with all the love and tenderness he had in his bursting heart once they were reunited. Maya had even quietened in his arms, much to his delight. It seemed everyone was quite startled at the situation in which they found themselves. But Elijah was dreaming big! Now that they were free he had but one thing on his mind: how to get back to

England. Suddenly, as they made their way deeper into the jungle alongside the natural passageway of the river, Elijah interrupted Matzika in order to declare his masterplan.

"We're leaving this place!" Elijah announced as they came to the river. "I have enough treasure to take us all back to England where we can live happily, away from this nightmare!"

Elijah had not read his audience; the crowd looked on aghast at his madness.

"Now, if I can just find the treasure... It's buried very near here, I'm sure of it. Someone help me!"

The rain would not desist: on and on it came, flooding everything their eyes could see. Adelita and Maya huddled sometimes in the trees for warmth. Their initial elation had now morphed into something far darker; they had worried looks on both of their faces.

Elijah saw their concern. He began to speak, but their faces grew graver still.

"You know it's winter now. It must be a year since my mother died and I arrived in this land. It has made me a changed man, as you see!"

Elijah twirled as though a showman. Adelita was quite shaken. She gripped the tree just for the strength to remain upright as the rain and Elijah's words tormented her emotional world.

"Soon we'll all be together in England, just you wait and see."

At this Elijah continued his search, but the rapidity and nature of his speech had left everyone worried. Having thrown off his bloody English uniform he searched up and down the riverside for his treasure, but it was as yet to no avail. The rain continued to fall, showing no pity for the tribespeople or their makeshift leader's outlandish mission.

Chapter Nineteen

The Shaman knew something was wrong. He sensed it in the air, in his gut, in his soul. When the night time came and he was resigned to his hut, he unwrapped his herbs in a panic. He placed them in the bowl, his hands shaking, but a vision would not emerge from whatever combination he tried.

Had his powers abandoned him in his plight? Was he now a blind man in an darkening world? What was the cause of this stirring deep within his soul? If it had been any other night he wouldn't have risked it, but the situation - his feelings - begged to receive answers.

Elijah's reappearance and the subsequent madness which followed did not speak well of his own future. The medicine man sadly considered his chances of living to see another day now that his allegiances were so depleted.

At the moment of his deepest wondering, the entrance to the hut burst open. The eyes of the Spanish soldier searched from the bowl to the face of the Shaman for an explanation.

"What witchcraft is occurring here? Come out, old man, and explain yourself!" The officer was screaming with fear and rage in the face of such insolence.

The Shaman, panicking, disposed of his tools and exited the hut.

"Nothing, nothing!" The Shaman employed his limited Spanish in his anxiety to appease the officers.

"That's a lie!! We know you have the eye of spirit! Were you casting spells?"

At this a commotion started and the chain of command was activated. Soon Captain Emmanuel, a vicious understudy to the absent Captain Carlos, was on the scene and hungry for information.

"What say you, old man? Were you practising sorcery on us?"

"No, no!" The Shaman knew his sky was darkening, so he began to argue at length in his native tongue.

His linguistic shift only angered the Spaniards: the medicine man was tied to a post and flogged as the slave he had become for his troubles. The soldiers feared killing him and the consequences it would bring, but they also needed to make it clear they would not tolerate the ancient ways being practised in their midst. As the lashes rained down with increasing ferocity the crowd that gathered became agitated.

"You're going to kill him!" came a native's cry at last, as the blood seeped from the Shaman's frame and withered muscles contorted upon the reception of each blow.

"This man has been practising his magic for too long!" retorted the officers and continued upon their quest to prove a brutal lesson.

Apart from the sting of the spiky whips on his flesh, the aspect of his peril which alarmed the Shaman most was his lack of vision. In pondering the blank response to all of his spiritual questions he felt his spirit drain of its will to live. The lashes continued to land upon broken flesh and the crowd decided it had had enough.

"Leave him alone!" came the cries. First from one, then many; all the disparate languages began to unite in their message.

The scene continued, the blood was pouring, the chorus of reprimands was soon unanimously orchestrated. Then suddenly the crowd took matters into their own hands. Swords were swung at and then stolen by the tribesmen, who had waited long enough for their anger to unfold. Before long there was a full-scale revolt and the beating had to be postponed while it was dealt with. In the commotion the Shaman's heart finally caved in and gave up on the process of living which had brought and taken in frequently inequal measures.

Nevertheless the fight was a bloody one. As women and children screamed, the native men formed one body, fighting as one for their existences despite tribal boundaries. The departure of Captain Carlos and his men earlier that day had meant that the Spanish reserves were depleted and this had not gone unnoticed by the tribesmen. They stormed the Captain's office easily and before long the very perimeters of the mine were being penetrated.

At the point of the greatest chaos Captain Carlos had returned from his bloody mission. He heard the commotion before he saw it; the screams of dying men, the roars of varying emotions. The guns, jewels and food had already been found, making it a more even match than was initially anticipated.

With rage in their eyes and hatred in their minds the tribesmen began to flee the scene, sprinting into the jungle with whatever they could carry to protect and nourish them. The Captain was aghast. He realised that he had returned to mayhem as he observed a fire raging in the camp and watched those who remained beg for mercy. But it was not good enough for the Captain, who opened fire indiscriminately until someone eventually put a bullet through him.

His journey to the spirit world was bound to be a troubled one, but in watching the Captain's blood seep onto the ground beneath him the natives saw only beauty. The carnage of the day spread into the clear night sky – plumes of smoke and ash descended on the surrounding area. For miles around people everywhere knew something serious had occurred.

The tribesmen were scattered, often alone and scared. No Spaniards lived to tell the tale, such was the vengeance of the natives. They fought for their lives with the skill and passion of warriors, ransacking their memories for the secrets to the art of war.

Though the indigenous people tried to replicate what they once had it was never the same. Small groups of escapees formed, but they were vulnerable to attack and hopelessly outnumbered. It was all they could do to form a relationship with the seemingly endless stream of invaders and hope for a peaceful conclusion.

Chapter Twenty

Back at the mine earlier in the day, Captain Carlos awoke from a nap. Rolling over and stretching, he returned to an upright position given a copious amount of time. His head hurt and his stomach felt full to bursting. Indeed, the officer wondered if he had been dreaming: he seemed to vaguely recall trading with a young Englishmen in a generous fashion and wanted to check it wasn't all for nothing.

The Spaniard went to the cabinet and withdrew the chest Mr. Cane had given him. He took the treasure out and inspected it, marvelling at the contours and markings. He scrutinised the details of each piece, one at a time, with a care that consumed his now sober mind. It suddenly occurred to him that some of the jewels looked familiar: the shapes, the small scratches, the features struck a chord. They were his own but weeks ago. The Captain nearly fell off his chair in shock when he realised he had been fooled and called instantly for his finest soldiers to gather and await his commands.

Outside the rain showed no compassion and continued to fall without interruption. Deep in the jungle Elijah was having trouble remembering the outlay of the land, the curves of the river – in truth, he could hardly see. As the Spaniards made their way through the jagged features of the land, heavily armed and intent on revenge, the rain dissuaded them from making progress. A few miles ahead Elijah, disorientated and foggy of mind, still could not find the burial place.

"Where is it? WHERE IS IT?" Elijah screeched into the chaos, too exhausted by his efforts and adrenaline to really catch his breath. Whether it was due to the ghastly weather or his loosening grip on sanity he could not recognise the features of the river for once in his life – as the raindrops lashed down every bend looked the same and the trees provided their plentiful camouflage all too well.

The groups collided in the midst of their respective journeys, the Spaniards finally catching up with the tribal people and their mad English friend. Shots were fired and, although the tribe fought back as well as they could, they were heavily outnumbered and swiftly gunned down.

Elijah, in his panic and mania, had not heard the enemy approaching and was shocked to find his awareness so lax. Ista, the straggler, was first to die. He had perched himself on the edge of the group, disheartened that Elijah had been willing to exchange him for another. Now the others watched as Ista took his final breath and fell face-forward into the river. Something told the tribesmen that they would not be far behind the young warrior. Mana was next, her female cries no deterrent for the cold-blooded Spaniards. With her wisdom and guile Elijah knew her soul would find its way to a better world than this.

Matzika and Elijah could barely see in the rain and Adelita moved closer to Elijah for protection. As she came towards him, though, a shot connected and went straight through her skull, sending her twisted, lifeless body spiralling to the floor.

After watching Adelita lose her life in front of him, Elijah began to scream. It was the wail of an animal, long tortured and finally defeated. The lashing rain, along with the senseless brutality of this world, had finally soaked through to his soul. Kneeling with his fists outstretched to the Gods, Elijah's desire to remain alive had suddenly been surpassed. He made an easy target, totally refusing to continue to put up a fight against the dark forces he had felt surrounded by at every twist and turn of this futile escapade.

Finally, Captain Carlos put him out of his misery, a clear mercy killing at this point. Matzika, the only remaining tribesman, soon followed. The Captain showed no regard for the innocence or guilt of his foes. He nodded his head at his kinsmen, who understood that the battle had been won.

Deeper still in the jungle, though merely a mile downriver, Portuguese soldiers walked over Elijah's treasure, the hollowness of the chest ringing underfoot.

Chapter Twenty One

After Elijah's scream was silenced, an eerie quiet gained control of the scene. The birds had all flown away when the shooting began; the only sound seemed to be the heavy breathing of Elijah's killer. Captain Carlos held a smoking pistol reserved for special occasions. The death of his enemies was sweet to the Spaniard and he savoured the taste.

Then he heard it, slow at first then much clearer: the simpering cries of Maya. The Captain walked slowly towards the sound, which came from a bundle of bloody blankets tied to the chest of her deceased mother.

For a second he knew not what to do. Should they take the child, raise it in civilisation? Should he call it his own? Should he put a bullet through her head to bring cessation to her obvious distress? The options arranged themselves before him. He reached down and freed Maya from her dead mother. She felt right in his arms, comforting her felt reciprocal. But she was by now crying once again.

"Shhh, little one. Shhhh! Uncle Carlos is here, please stop this crying."

287

"Shall we go?" said one of the Spanish men who had assisted in the rampage.

"We cannot take a crying child with us. Who knows who she will alert to our presence?"

Maya sensed something terrible was happening all around her and there were screams now pouring from her mouth. The Captain felt his temper fraying. He looked around at the blood-pattered faces of his men, not a single clue between the whole lot of them. Infuriated now, Carlos took Maya to the edge of the river.

"May Christ bless and keep you," the officer said as he laid the baby in the violent current. As with her mother and father before her, Maya's suffering was soon to be no more.

Postscript

Over time many wars were fought for the jungle, its resources and surrounding territories: lines slowly alternated on wildly incorrect maps for years to come. The turbulent tides of rebellions and uprisings left all dizzy; peace was but a rumour people heard through the years.

It took centuries for the countries to form: Argentina, Columbia, Brazil and all besides forming fixed identities, cultures and connections. An uneasy calm settled over the landscapes which had been a stage for some of the most savage and beautiful moments the human species had ever experienced.

The indigenous people continued their retreat into the deepest regions of the jungle, even as it was slowly stripped of its layers and stood naked in parts for all of humanity to see the shame that greed had brought upon the world.

Christianity continued its march into unventured territories, all but a few escaping the options Christ provided for them. To this day indigenous people all across the world have to fight for their culture, land and lives in the face of outright racism, theft, rape and murder. This, so they say, is civilisation.

All those involved in the fray had their individual journeys irrespective of their position in the wider whole. In the shade beneath the tree of non-existence, most of the souls that departed this world were filled with the same sense of remorse, relief and hopelessness. Each spirit formed a part of a puzzle that was beyond human understanding; the meaning escaped even the brightest minds, who were humble in the face of infinite wisdom.

The pieces of the puzzle held by the native people - the love for the Earth, their harmony with the natural world and, at times, one another - are indeed hunted qualities in today's world. Everywhere ideologies such as these are found they are stifled and eradicated, even in the young. At some point during the human journey survival became a notion seemingly frowned upon by intellectuals.

Elijah's soul reached towards the light in the same worn out condition as the others. All his attempts at greatness - perhaps even holiness - had fallen short of their intended target. A good man he was not, but a free man he had been born and a free man he eventually died. All between was a battle he could finally claim to have won: his liberty was his only virtue, right to the very end.

Captain Carlos had expected to meet Christ as his priests had insisted he would, but emerged in the spirit world to find himself consigned to the shabbier quarters of the afterlife. The tribal people and their invaders all jostled for position among the awesomeness of the spiritual realm, order kept in place by the same forces that governed the elements that Elijah so bowed down before during his initial experience at the peak of the sacred mountain.

Little had he known that fleeting glimpse of understanding would be all he was apportioned in his short life: the rest was a maelstrom of desperation and confusion. Only in dying could some of the answers he sought be found.

Others weren't so fortunate as to know them. Back in the mortal realm the coming of progress signalled the making of slaves right across the New World. Millions were taken from their homes, too many to ever be able to definitively count. Forced to live under the invaders' guidance, those from Africa and beyond were imported to the Americas to forward the notion of a society in which native people were mostly born into suffering. Its legacy remains prominent today.

All around this troubled modern world there is a yearning for a brighter tomorrow. The cries of the women and children alone have been going on too long to be continually ignored. The great leaders who have spoken out against the crimes committed by their fellow men have all been silenced one way or another, and the human species continues to be led by foolish manipulators which the innocents have done nothing to deserve.

The world which Elijah foresaw has indeed come to pass. Times of struggle and quiet desperation have found the human race, the wars and their leaders regularly rearranging. The religious point to the prophesies of the end times, illuminating what would otherwise be a dark world with their glimmers of understanding a hint of a masterplan. But is the light artificial? How long can it be clung to?

In time perhaps a harmony will return to the Earth, like the coming of day at the end of a particularly long night. But for now humanity struggles and strives under the weight of its own expectations, shackles rearranging and slave masters alternating in the cruel and pernicious system of existence which has come to dominate almost the entire world.

When will it end? No one knows.
Who is responsible? Every living being.
What must be done? We must choose love.
Will we prevail? Let's see.

Printed in Great Britain
by Amazon